# The Cheat Code
# for God Mode

THE NEW BIZARRO AUTHOR SERIES
PRESENTS

# The Cheat Code for God Mode

Andy de Fonseca

Eraserhead Press
Portland, OR

ERASERHEAD PRESS
205 NE BRYANT
PORTLAND, OR 97211

WWW.ERASERHEADPRESS.COM

ISBN: 978-1-62105-126-8

# Editor's Note:

Welcome to the New Bizarro Author Series. This is Andy de Fonseca's first book. I first "met" her when she was my student in an online writing workshop that I taught with Eraserhead Press author Garrett Cook (I think she won a free class by attending a reading with bizarro authors in Chicago). Since I'm easily bored by fight scenes, there's an exercise that I like to do with my students in which I ask them to write scenes that are extremely entertaining and unique. Andy wrote about a monk who decides to practice pandamancy (look it up) and the terrible consequences that happen as a result of it. I was impressed, so later when I first started seeking authors to write books for the New Bizarro Author Series, I sent her an email. And it ended up being a joy to work with her and her gleeful enthusiasm

Now let's talk about the series: it's designed to test the waters for new bizarro authors to see if they have what it takes to find a readership. It's up to you as far as whether or not Eraserhead Press will be publishing more of Andy's books in the future. To succeed, she must sell several hundred copies of this book over the next year. So if you like this book, I encourage you to tell your friends about it and write a review (particularly for Amazon).

Thanks so much for giving this book a chance. I hope you enjoy it as much as I enjoyed editing it.

~~Bradley Sands

*Dedicated to the men in my life:*

Tim White, my dad who is always laughing
John Moore, my step-dad who always had stories to tell
Myles, my amazing husband
Michael Allen Rose, my biggest cheerleader
Greg Cliff, the nicest guy I know, like, seriously
Mike Kesler, my token Alpha Male
Lecester Reed, my resident superhero geek
Bradley Sands, one incredibly patient editor

*Special Thanks To:*

The Internet.
Because dayum, bitch, you cray!

# Chapter One

## The Ups & Downs of Antiquing

"The Japanese win for most fucked-up inventions of all time," Margy said, tossing a portable toilet belt back on a table covered in useless junk. The tiny loo landed in a pile of tangled phone chargers, robotic animal toys, and hair-growing dolls whose locks were spilling to the floor. The dolls seemed like a good idea at the time of invention, for little girls going through the phase of chopping manes, but the box omitted telling parents that the hair didn't *stop* growing. Now there were landfills of nothing but hair. Japan had made an amusement park out of it.

Victor didn't look up from a turticorn (an unfortunate experiment from a child's *Clone Me, Splice Me!*™ set) floating in a tank too small for its shell and horn. "Should we check out the sex dolls again? I hear if you program them right, they can be battle-bots."

"I'm a little worried that would end up being just one giant, angry orgy."

"That's not a bad thing," Victor said. "We could sell tickets."

"That market's already saturated."

Margy continued down the congested aisle of the antique shop, glancing around the overcrowded shelves. Seeing no end to the clutter she didn't care about, she shouted toward the front, "Len! Where'd you move your games?"

Through a wall of discarded, rotting books, she heard a muffled, "Corner left."

Victor followed Margy to the back of the shop, picking up a jellyfish farm kit for examination. "So what happened to hanging out with your old classmates? Weren't you going to try to make some new connections?"

9

"Whatever," Margy replied. "They were douchebags."

"How?"

"The way they talked."

"I think you just can't make friends."

They looked through the stack of games made for various systems that went back to the beginning of gaming history. Cartridges, discs, minidiscs, cards, minicards, and slivers piled to the ceiling.

"What about *MarksHunter 4: Return to Swamp River*?"

Margy shook her head. "My Opus system's going out, remember?"

"Fix it, woman."

"Not for a *MarksHunter* game. Their graphics got worse with each sequel. Not worth my time finding such old parts."

"Man, you suck."

Margy shrugged and grabbed a chair to check the top of the stack.

Victor eyed a minidisc. "So, how was work today?"

"Lame."

"Unusual. What's up?"

"They hired a bunch of new broads."

Victor ooed. "I hope they're hot."

"I *hope* they're qualified and help out. Besides, what's it matter to you? Aren't you dating someone?"

"Ehhh... she's in that threesome phase...."

Margy gave an understanding nod and they searched through the games. She rolled her eyes as she read the back descriptions while Victor quietly mumbled them to himself. Each time they pulled out a new game, the heap threatened to topple. Victor finally straightened.

"If you're not going to fix your Opus, I don't see anything new. And I'm hungry. And my feet hurt. And whine."

She put down the game she was reading. "Fine. After you."

Just as Victor stepped away, he let out a shrill yelp and fell to the floor, followed by the stack of games.

10

After the crash settled, Margy sighed. "Nice."

Len, a balloon-shaped man in glasses, came running back. "Now what'd you do?"

Margy huffed. "Nothing, if you'd clean up your junk palace—" she grabbed the cord Victor had tripped on and yanked it up, "—and didn't leave it looking like a shit hole all the—"

"Calm down, Margy." Len held up a hand. "Just clean up the games—"

"Your store, your mess."

"Margy!" Victor squealed. His sparkling, schoolgirl eyes were fixated on what she held in her hand. The mangled cord she grasped connected to a light blue orb with a single button and thin slot. "A NarviPlay!"

"When did you get this?" Margy demanded.

Len pulled out a small remote, pressed a button, and up popped a bright screen. He tapped in the name. "NarviPlay. Twenty-five years ago, September second."

"We come here every other week, Len!" Margy shot. "Where the hell's it been?"

"Doesn't matter!" Victor jumped up, scrambling to straighten and restack the games. "Are there controllers and how much?"

Len glanced at the screen. "Should be four controllers, and hell, I've had it for so long. Five credits."

"Three."

Victor nudged her. "Give him a break!"

"We don't even know if it works."

"Whatever," Len growled. "Three credits. Just pay and get out before real customers come in and Margy pisses them off somehow."

Victor pressed his thumbprint on the screen, Len handed them their bag, and Margy stepped out the door.

Jupiter blanketed the east sky as the sun set westward, washing the streets in a heavy orange aura. Victor stared at the Great Red Spot on the planet in front of him. "I've seen it every day of my life and I still worry someday I'm going to jump too high and be sucked in."

Margy glanced at the giant, centuries-old storm of Jupiter for a moment before starting down the street. "I'm surprised it hasn't happened already."

They walked past the long lines for the motus-aers, which flashed every few seconds, leaving the silver discs on the ground empty. The next person stepped on, clicked to their destination, and in a flash of white, was gone.

"I'm happy to see more of those popping up," Victor smiled. "Seemed to take forever for the town council to approve them."

"The vote was between preserving the historical downtown area as an accurate replica and having the ability to be even more lazy. Which would you choose?"

"Lazy, of course. If it weren't for you, I'd be hopping those block to block."

"Of course." Margy stopped. "Walk along the river," she said, looking to her other side, "or walk along the city?"

Victor looked at the peaceful river and the trees slightly swaying in the breeze. He turned to the other side. Mere feet after the edge of the downtown area, skyscrapers covered in foliage disappeared into the clouds. Crop pickers suspended by a line of wire walked down the sides of the buildings, filling their bags.

"River. It's shorter, and less chance of people falling on you."

They made their way past the historic homes, cut through a mini-mall dedicated to body part replacement (*"for humans* and *their lovable pets!"*), and slid through the gate of the old elementary school playground as a shortcut. The abandoned lot hadn't been connected to a school for nearly twenty years, but could never be deconstructed as it was made out of wormholes and glowing portals. A few pieces of playground equipment were ignored during the move and dotted the grounds.

A group of zoomos were hanging out on the jungle gym, their animal paws easily grasping the bars as they hung upside down and swung about. They were human by all means other than their outer shells being those of an upright animal.

"So then," Victor continued a story, "the receptionist was yakking on her remote being like, '*How'm I doin'? It's MONDAY, guuuuurl*'. She doesn't *do* anything, Margy! Nothing about Monday makes it any different than the rest of the week. It's like a desk lamp saying, 'Oh, shit. It's Monday!' Like, yes, desk lamp, and you'll do the same minorly useful task you do every other day of the week."

"I'm sure she's a vital part to your data office," Margy said.

"The receptionist role was replaced decades ago by the infranet and common sense. It's better than a receptionist because you're always connected, *without* having to listen to elevator music and someone hate their life. That's the beauty of the system." Victor shifted his bag. "People order their familiars online, we get the order through email, the order is fulfilled. End of transaction."

A loud shout caused the two to halt their conversation and turn back to the group on the playground. A cat-person came running up to them on two legs with speed, grace, and determination.

"You're Margy, right?" the cat-woman asked, her pointed ears twitching.

"Yes," she replied, not inviting a conversation.

"Hi. I'm Mau."

"The Egyptian goddess of cats? That's not obvious."

Mau's smile faltered but she pushed through. "You work at the planetarium, right?"

"Yes."

Mau motioned to the other animal-people behind her. "We all were wondering if there was a way we could check the place out after hours. Just to get a closer look at that pop-up projection you guys have. It's really a thing of beauty."

"No."

The cat huffed. "Why not!"

"Because I don't know you. And no, in general."

Mau's hair stood on end and her pupils dilated. "I see. Racist against zoomos, huh?"

"She's not," Victor cut in. "She hates everyone equally."

"It's true."

Mau's tail relaxed but she still stood stiff. She turned and made her way back to her group of animal friends.

"Man..." Victor grumbled, "could you at least *try* not to be such a raging bitch to everyone? She was hot."

"You obviously have shit taste, Victor. But that's fine."

As Victor and Margy stepped off the school's lot, angry howling, grunting, and yipping could be heard.

"That reminds me," Victor said. "Want to visit the elephant pit tomorrow?"

Margy continued on. "Watching large animals stuck in suspended gravity is an activity I don't ever want to have time for."

Back at Victor's place, an 8-bit chicken served Margy a bowl of chips as she sat on the floor with the NarviPlay in her lap and the cord between her fingers. She squeezed the wire cutters and pulled back the casing.

"And who is this one?" Margy asked, taking the bowl from the pixelated poultry.

"That's Mort!" Victor smiled. "I designed him myself. What do you think?"

"He's terrible. Who wants a chicken as their familiar? And I've seen you make them with way better design. This is just confusing."

Victor shook his head as he poured a beer. "Nah, I wanted the old school look. And no one's going to steal a chicken."

The 8-bit Mort nestled in its padded bed next to the couch.

"What abilities did you give him?"

"Detect, forgery, and flight." Margy raised an eyebrow. "They deserve a chance to fly." He put a mug of lager next to Margy and took a spot on one of the large foam balls he had found in a thrift store. "So, do we even have a game for this system?"

"No. And shit, because I doubt we'll find one. There were only twenty games released with this thing before it was cancelled."

Victor watched over her shoulder as she fixed the wires. "How are the episodes?"

Margy was silent for several moments, intently stripping the copper wiring. "I had one a week ago. Woke up in someone's fountain wearing all black with my hair cut short."

"Oh, yeah. I thought you just got sick of long hair."

"I guess I did, because I don't even remember doing it." She rolled the cord casing back and taped it up, next grabbing the small screwdriver and pulling the orb close. "They've been happening more frequently than before and I'm just worried that—" She cut herself off and lifted the top of the orb.

Victor stared at his drink. "Is this how it started with your parents?"

Margy pulled out a small metal piece in the game system. "Do you have a 50KX here? This one's shot."

"No. You took my only extra for your Opus. Go get it from there."

"I don't want to go all the way home."

"It's across the street!"

"Too far. Do your parents have one?"

"How should I know?"

"They live across the hall. Go ask. And if they don't, pull one from a system we haven't used in a while."

Margy continued to tinker with the game system's inner workings until Victor came back with a small metal plate. She screwed the top back on, plugged the cord into an adapter, and pressed the small, lone button.

Victor punched the air as the orb glowed like a child's moon toy. Mort growled.

"Um," Margy said.

"Ignore that. Glitch I need to fix."

A screen lit up in front of a blank wall with a NarviPlay logo illuminating the room. There was a small click.

"Still broken!" Victor teased.

Margy's glare was cut short when a disc ejected from the sphere.

"We lucked out there." Victor grabbed the minidisc. "*Adamina*. Know it?"

"Only that it had a small cult following." She pulled out her small pocket remote, pushed a button, and typed onto the screen that popped up. "A low-budget, independent sandbox game modeled after the world. The *entire* world."

"Was it the first one to do that?"

Margy scanned the description. "Looks like shovelware. *Adamina*'s graphics were shite and not many could find the point. Says the commands in the menu were difficult to figure out as far as actually doing anything fun."

"Sounds like a bunch of babies who didn't know what they were doing."

"If comments on review sites tell us anything, then yes, that's exactly it."

Victor ran his finger along the disc. "There are numbers scribbled onto this."

"Whatever. Pop in the disc. Let's play."

He studied the numbers a bit longer before slipping the disc back into the thin slot. A loud whirring filled the orb. There was a jump, and the whirring stopped. Margy inhaled deeply, but before she could utter a sound, the disc began to spin again. The orb glowed green and a crackling image sputtered onto the screen. *ADAMINA* dropped into view. A menu screen pulled up with options.

> *One player*
> *Multiplayer*

Margy grabbed a controller. "You want to play?"
"Count me in."

> *Controller*
> *Glasses & Glove*

"Suck," Victor moped. "We could've done VR."

*Type Your City & State*

16

Margy ferociously punched in the name of their town.

S-P-R-I-N-K-L-E-S-B-U-R-G-H

I-N

An avatar creator popped on screen and she hit enter to choose default.

"Don't you want it to look like you?" Victor asked, carefully choosing his avatar's haircut.

"If I can't make an avatar instantly by just taking a photo, I don't care."

Victor shrugged and took another ten minutes to pick an outfit. His boxy character wore a bright green shirt and textureless black pants.

"You don't have a goatee," Margy said.

"I would if I could grow one."

She hit enter again and the screen dissolved into darkness. A talk box outlined in glowing light blue popped up. Letters and numbers began to type themselves out.

*V2VsY29tZSB0byBjb21tYW5kIGNlbnRlci44g*

Another talk box appeared as a reply, and the same odd language responded.

*V2hlcmUgYW0gST8NCg==*

*WW91IGNhbiBjb250cm9sIHRoZSB3b3JsZCBmcm9tIGhlcmUu*

*SG93Pw==*

*WW91IGllc3QgZmluZCBhbiBlcXVhdGlvbi4g*

They vanished, and more boxes glowed onto the screen and quickly left.

"Hey!" Victor tried slapping the controller out of Margy's hand. "Quit clicking past it! That's dialogue, we may need it."

"Meh. It has elements of an old programming script. It wouldn't be worth the research."

She continued to click past until the screen went black again. A low hum built up from nothing and hit the bottom of their stomachs, crescendoing to vibrate each vertebrae before stopping at the top of their spines. Shortly later, a dim light appeared in the corner and a man in a tuxedo walked into the spot. His large mouth opened and stayed open for several seconds before a small text box arose from the darkness. One by one, words glimmered onto the screen before quickly going out:

*The world is* yours *to bear.*
*The choices you make are the* world's *to bear.*

*Be courteous.*
*Be divine.*
*Be careful.*

# Chapter Two

## Of Heroes & Hot Dogs

Sprinklesburgh appeared before them in choppy, pixelated obscurity. The downtown district sat sans detail with only the rough outlines of buildings discernable enough for navigation. A jagged sound effect of flowing water filled Victor's apartment, peaking several moments throughout the loop. Generic conversation between strangers was overly joyous. Overall, it was indeed their town, but dated and drab.

"Gross," Margy complained. "Polygons? Texture mapping? And look at these edges. You'd think this game came out before anti-aliasing."

"It's not that bad, Margy," Victor said patiently. "Look, the pre-rens are really nice. It was a small, independent game–"

"The clipping! Oh, their gods, the clipping!"

"Oy. Ignore the graphics. Go find a mission."

Margy hopped on Victor's avatar before running up to a street character in a plain white dress. She hit A to start a conversation.

*Hi, how are you?*

*Thank you.*

*The weather pleases you?*

*I love the rain.*

*Should we get to know each other?*

*All Tuesdays.*

"Oh, fuck me," Margy twitched. "This is terrible. Give me a plot point!"

"What if it's straight sandbox?"

"Then I'll search street view on the infranet and get perfect resolution."

"Maybe we're not talking to the right people."

They ran their avatars down the streets of their duplicate town for someone interesting, but kept seeing the same five people scattered throughout.

Victor frowned. "I think there are two cars rendered in this game."

"Hold up. Checking out menu screen."

Four small boxes popped up: a miniscule map, a command center, and two health and inventory logs for each avatar. Margy entered a command.

>*Giant chicken*

The command center closed and a two-dimensional, regular-sized chicken appeared on screen, unmoving. It flickered for a moment before disappearing.

"What bullox," Margy grunted. "*Mort* is better than that."

"Insults! There's no comparison!" Victor moved his avatar. "Let's go see what my place looks like in polygon form."

Victor ran his avatar down the streets, through the mini-malls, and across the playground.

"There it is." He knocked on the apartment's red door and waited. His avatar knocked again.

Shortly later, a woman in a plain white dress answered.

*Hello. How may I help you?*

"Yeah," Victor nodded. "This is shit. No wonder no one played it."

"We should try throwing her to the street. Maybe that will get an original response."

"You could break her neck!"

Margy shrugged. "Not my problem."

*I love the rain.*

"Look," Victor stood, "you play with it for a bit. I have to hunt the wild poo."

"The most dangerous game."

Victor left the room and Mort tried running after him. As Victor shut the bathroom door, it bounced back, and there was a loud bark. "Whoops, sorry, Mort!" He closed the door and Mort continued to bark outside it.

Margy ran her avatar down the street but was stopped by a wall of foliage. She ran it down another street, turned down another, and was stopped by a tall brick wall.

"There's nothing to do!"

She opened the menu screen again and entered into the command center.

>*Mission*

Nothing.

>*Walk through walls*

Nothing.

>*Battle*

Nothing.

>*Car*

A car materialized in front of her character and she hopped in. She tried driving off road, but at the curb the car stopped immediately, making a dull *thud*. She reversed and tried again, driving into a person. The car again stopped and made a dull *thud*, then the person walked away from the minor annoyance.

>*FUCK YOU FUCKING FUCK*

The screen twitched and two poorly designed, naked characters appeared, awkwardly gyrated toward each other for a couple moments, and disappeared.

"I think I pulled an ass muscle," Victor said, stepping into the room, Mort at his feet. "Anything?"

Margy threw the controller at the screen, only for it to hit the wall behind it.

"It's just not the same anymore with projector displays," Victor sighed.

Margy hit the button on the NarviPlay and grabbed the minidisc. "We should make it our mission to destroy all *Adamina*s." She clutched the disc to snap it in half, but froze.

"Victor, these letters and numbers. They're actually scribbled on here."

"Yeah, I told you that. There you go not listening again."

"I thought you meant it was the design of the disc. Not something an actual player put on here." She pulled out her remote, clicked the button, held up the disc behind the screen, and took a picture.

She shoved the disc back in the slot, picked up her controller, and clicked past the dialogue and menus until she came to the command center.

>*Cheat*

Nothing.

>*Cheat Menu*

Nothing.

>*Cheat Code*

A large box appeared with only a blinking underscore. Margy opened the photo of the disc and copied the code, letter by letter, number by number.

*SW5pdGlhdGUgR29kIE1vZGUuIERvd25sb2F
kLiBJbW1vcnRhbGl0eS4gTWFwIGhhY2tpbmc
uIFdhbGwgaGFja2luZy4gQm9vc3Rpbmcu IEZ
1bGwgbW9uZXkuIEVudmlyb25tZW50IGNvbn
Ryb2wuIEZlbGwgQ3JlYXRpb24uIFNjcmlwdGl
uZy4=*

The screen flashed a bright, luminous blue. Small text typed itself out in the bottom left-hand corner.

*God Mode Activated*

The screen went black.
Long moments passed.
"Not much of a God Mode," Victor mumbled.
A bar blinked on screen.

*Downloading updated information...*

Victor and Margy watched as pixel by pixel, bit by bit, their downtown district developed into a highly-detailed, extremely precise version of how it looked today. The streets were filled with cars of every model, objects reacted to the wind blowing in the game, and people—each one unique—chatted along the sidewalks with their familiars close by.

Last to be downloaded was the playable avatar. The name above his full health bar read "OP."

"What kind of name is OP?"

Margy glanced at it. "Original Player."

She opened the menu and the pathetic few boxes that were there before were now replaced with a world of information. The map showed an entire universe with a mini map off to the side pinpointing OP's place in it. The single inventory box was full of categories for items available. The health bar glowed at maximum capacity. Another box blinked: *CONNECT TO INTERNET FOR UPDATED WORLD NEWS.*

"That's weird," Margy said, "aren't we already connected to the infranet?"

"Yeah…" Victor agreed cautiously. "Isn't everything? It should automatically link up to the infranet by just existing."

Margy shook her head, selected the command box, and entered text.

>*Mission*

*Save the world.*
*However you see fit.*

Margy groaned. "So we just play around until something needs to be saved?" She handed the controller over to Victor. "I'm the last person the world wants as a designated hero."

"Maybe it's like, a morality game. *Who do you save when two are threatened! Who are the real bad guys! Shoot the hostage!*"

She rolled her eyes. "I say we just get in a car and run over some hookers."

"In!"

"Snatch us a nice car, please. I'll be your Miss Daisy."

OP hopped in front of a smoothly driving Jaguar, which instantly stopped. The jolted driver honked relentlessly. Victor moved OP to yank open the door, rip out the driver, and toss him to the curb.

"Hey-o, you have an audience!" Margy chimed. "Better head out. He probably hit his panic button on you."

"How nice! I need a good bull chase."

Victor ran the red at the intersection, nicking cars, obliterating a bench, and taking out a Civil War era replica light pole. Familiars dotted the front windshield like bugs. Victor spritzed them and turned on the wipers.

"Man, look at those people dive," Margy smiled. "They're way better at not dying in this game than others. Maybe that'll be a challenge later."

"Hot dog bot! Hot dog bot!" Victor accelerated and hot dogs went flying.

Sirens filled the air. Red and blue lights flickered off buildings.

"Finally. Response time is way slow in this game."

Victor sped down the historic streets and onto the multilayer highway as two more bulls joined the chase. Ever since the zoomos appeared, police officers around the world were replaced with those in stronger, more effective bodies. Those bodies happened to be in the shapes of humanoid wolves, bears, and most of the time—bulls.

"Take the portal to Walnut and Riverside!"

Tires screeched as OP's car cut across the lanes and slipped through the glowing blue portal, immediately exiting onto a busy street in another part of town.

Margy jumped. "Go by foot, lose them in the hospital parking garage."

Victor crashed into the garage, his car plowing through a line of vehicles. OP dove out of the crumbled Jaguar unscathed and started running. The circular parking garage rose into the sky and OP jumped from level to level, easily gliding upwards.

"The fuzz are behind you, it's the running of the bulls!"

OP was eight stories high when he started sprinting, only to be stopped by a bull already there. Both were frozen, with OP at the other end of a large double barrel.

"What's your action button do?" Margy asked.

Victor jumped out of the line of fire and hit X. OP's arms stretched out and from his hands, thumbtacks and pushpins shot forward, pricking the bull, who was more agitated than hurt.

Victor grunted and OP ran. "Why would the last player *ever* need *that* as a weapon?"

The bull grabbed OP's collar and landed a heavy punch. OP was unfazed and grabbed the bull by the horns. Without effort, he sent the bull flying across the garage. OP continued his run.

"You think we'll hurt OP if we make him jump?"

Margy shook her head. "God Mode, we can do whatever we…what the hell is that?"

A green orb with wings fluttered into view. A conversation box appeared.

*Hey! Hey listen! Hey! Listen to me!*

"Is that his familiar?" Victor asked.

Shots were fired and OP fell to the ground, blood splattered the concrete but quickly disappeared. Purple goo from the bullet dripped onto his hand. The health bar remained full.

"Shit!" Margy hit Victor. "That green thing's going to get us caught. Jump off the garage and get out of there."

The glowing ball with wings disappeared. There was a herd of bulls now, all running toward OP.

Victor jumped OP over the edge. The avatar hit the ground and rolled for several yards before easily standing and bolting away from the scene.

"Did you see any experience points get added to anything?" Victor asked.

"No. Maybe it's in the start screen."

He shrugged. "Whatever. I'm done with this. Let's try something else." He opened the command center.

>*invisible*
>*womens bath house*

Margy rolled her eyes. "I sometimes forget you have a sex drive."

The setting around OP evaporated and in its place pale pink marble formed. The faint outline of OP could be seen as Victor moved him throughout the steamy lavation room.

Victor stared through glassy eyes. "How could people find this game pointless?"

Margy was unamused. "You make even fake things creepy."

"Look, Margy, look," Victor giggled. "I can walk through walls."

OP ran through several occupied shower pods lined up through the middle of the room.

"Margy, if you weren't here, this would be one of the happiest moments of my life."

Margy stuck out her tongue in disgust. "I can fix that for you." Head in hand, she watched OP jump through a wall and into the sauna, where several bare females—human and zoomo—leaned back in relaxation. Their skin glistened with the moisture in the air, their cheeks blushed from the heat, and sweat drops dripped down their curves.

"I still don't see a point in this game other than it being a virtual stalker for the sick and perverted."

"Shhhhh... you're ruining it."

"And I'm out." Margy stood.

"Oh, Margy, don't be like that!" Except Victor didn't look away from the screen.

"Tomorrow, when you run out of lotion or your hand starts cramping, let me know. Let's do lunch."

"I have the stamina of a steroid-induced ox, you won't hear from me for a week."

"Blech."

Shortly later, the door shut with Mort barking after her.

# Chapter Three

## Imagination Abomination

Mr. Vance spooned a heaping helping of scrambled eggs onto Victor's plate while Mrs. Vance scrolled through the news on the small screen in front of her. Victor was engrossed in a hard copy of a comic that sat next to him.

"What a waste of trees," Mrs. Vance mumbled.

"You used to read these, mom, come on."

"The colors are more vibrant on a screen and your eyes aren't strained as much."

"Don't argue with him so early, Lys. Not when there are other things going on."

"I'm not arguing, *Johnny, sweetheart, sugar cane*. But why waste money–"

"That reminds me," Johnny smiled. "Victor, leave your place unlocked today if you head out. Lys and I are going to look through your NineX games."

"Don't you know the code?" Victor asked.

"You always seem to change it," Lyssa said with no real concern. Behind her, their familiar—a rounded, five-pointed star with eyes—floated in front of the stove, flipping the bacon. "What kind is that?"

"The bacon?" Johnny asked, turning to it. "Turtle, why?"

Lyssa sighed. "Please stop doing that. They're flying rodents, I don't want to eat that."

"Science said they're fine."

"It's disgusting."

"Well, you shouldn't've eaten the eggs then, either." Johnny smiled again. Lyssa took in a deep breath to yell but was interrupted. "You and Margy didn't happen to be downtown when shit hit the fan yesterday, were you, Victor?"

28

Victor didn't look up. "Huh?"

"Oh, honey, try to read the news," Lyssa said, exhaling. "An unstable escaped yesterday, wreaking complete havoc. I know you two like to go down there after work on Fridays. Did either of you happen to see anything?"

Victor flipped a page. "Nope. Pretty boring per usual." The floating star dropped flying-turtle bacon onto Victor's plate.

"Those poor unstables. It wouldn't be so bad if at least *someone* was trying to figure out what happened to them." Lyssa turned back to Johnny, who was sitting down. "Says here the bulls almost had him at the hospital."

Margy stared incredulously at the girl, unable to comprehend the words that were being vomited before her:

"And then I thought for sure it was okay, right? Because he said yeah sure and why not and I didn't know him, right? But if we do it why not and no harm done and–"

"So wait," Margy cut her off. "I get called into work, on a Saturday, because you don't even have the common sense to lead a tour group through the planetarium without fucking it up?"

The girl opened her mouth to respond, closed it, and opened it again. "I...I do have common sense, right? But I thought it was a thing of the planetarium, right? To allow private tours–"

"Yeah, I don't care. Not in the slightest. You're fired. Congratulations on breaking the record for shortest amount of time in employment. We'll be sure to have a plaque made up."

"Just listen to me!"

"No. Because I still don't care."

"But–"

"If caring was a fiery ball of plasma, mine would be a black hole so deep and large not even the universe itself would remain intact."

The girl's eyes filled with tears.

"In a contest about not caring, I would easily sweep the competition, win several gold medals, and be talked about for decades in the annals of not caring history."

"You've made your–"

"If not caring were a hot dog," Margy drilled, "my hot dog would make God full."

She wiped her eyes. "You're such a bitch."

"That may hurt if I respected you." The girl grabbed her bag and ran out. Margy pinched the bridge of her nose. "Bitter irony that someone who hates stupid people as much as I do would end up working in conjunction with several...." She turned to another new girl sitting in the break room and noticed her foxtail and ears. Her pointed snout was short and smooth.

"Erin, can I trust your judgment on leading tours?"

"Of course," the fox replied, her voice serene. "I'm not a complete moron."

The faintest of smiles appeared on Margy's face before it was interrupted by a loud news anchor on the projected screen in the corner of the room.

*"Sources say the man was chased to the hospital parking garage where he left his stolen car, jumped level to level, and ran across the eighth-story deck. Five bulls followed him, but they are now seeing psychiatric doctors. Here's a clip from yesterday."*

The screen cut to a shaking bull in uniform, damp with cold sweat, towering over the anchor.

*"He ran at incredible speed.... We caught him on the eighth floor, just standing there, staring off.... Then he jumped. He* [beep] *jumped."* It was awkward seeing a grown bull cry. *"We ran over... and the* [beep] *stood! He ran a few yards and then just... he just..."*

*"What happened, sir?"*

The bull looked at the news anchor. No emotion. No flinching. *"He vanished."*

Margy burst through Victor's door. He shrieked and the comic ripped in two. Mort barked relentlessly.

"News!"

Victor didn't wait to be told twice and hit the remote. They watched a collage of multiple apps report on the carjacking, the unstable driver, the obliterated hot dog bot, and the growing number of sources that had seen a jumping man survive an eight-story fall and disappear.

"Coincidence," Victor said, sounding unsure of himself. Margy shook her head.

"Turn the game on."

*Adamina* glowed onto the screen and OP appeared on a street corner. Margy picked up the controller and led him through the streets. Down Main Street. Through the mini-mall. Across the school playground. OP turned onto Middle Street. He ran past several recognizable homes. He stood in front of an apartment complex. OP moved to the red door.

A knocking reverberated throughout Victor's apartment. Margy dropped the controller. They both stared at the door.

# Chapter Four

## 神モードが作動した。

Margy yanked the cord from the wall. Victor balled onto the floor and grabbed his head.

"What have we done what have we done what have we done!"

"Breathing exercises."

"Hee hee hooooo. Hee hee hooooo. We destroyed property! Hee hee hooooo. Stole a car! Hee hee—DID WE KILL ANYONE?"

Margy's breath escaped her as she stared at the NarviPlay, the orb casting a light blue circle on the floor where the sun went through it. She pulled out her remote and turned on her screen. She searched the apps.

"No... but there were injuries. Lots of damage."

"We have to fix this!"

"Let's be positive it's our fault! This is impossible, so it must have been someone, something else." She grabbed the cord but Victor slapped it out of her hand.

"We can't hurt more people! And it's not the most brilliant idea to send OP back out there when his face is on every local–"

"It's not." Margy brought up the different news apps on the big screen, which were reporting on the footage from various security cameras along the unstable's path. Each shot of OP was blurred or distorted.

"That's some lame movie cop out, there," Victor breathed.

"It's gotta be part of the cheat code."

Victor pulled himself to the couch. "Fine. Test it. But it has to be indisputable, and you can't hurt anyone, or destroy anything. No damage."

Margy nodded and plugged the cord into the wall. She grabbed the controller and sat next to Victor. OP appeared on a street corner. Margy opened the command center.

> *Giant chicken*

*[Enter]*

Nothing happened on screen. Victor and Margy waited. Then waited some more.

Victor put his head in his hands and stared at the coffee table. The stale lager in the mug from last night rippled ever so slightly.

It rippled again, stronger this time. Victor nudged Margy.

They felt it in their feet.

Margy looked at Victor. "A trash truck moving–"

The walls trembled. Victor jumped up. "I thought I said no destroying anything!"

He ran out the door with Margy close behind and sprinted to the end of the street. Down the road, at the end of Main Street, the river reflected the blinding sun, which failed to hinder the giant chicken that was wading through it. The chicken's wingspan easily stretched from south bank to north bank. Its feathers fluttered in the wind, water rushed around its bony yellow legs, and its red waddles flopped back and forth with each step. Crowds had gathered as far as their eyes could see.

"Turn the game off, Margy!"

She ran back and hit the button, ejecting the disc. Shortly later, Victor shut the door behind him.

"What happened?" Margy asked, afraid to breathe until she knew it was safe.

He was silent for several moments. Victor was sweating as if he had just ran a marathon. He shivered as if it were below freezing. He held on to the doorknob as though he would collapse. "It disappeared.... Like, a cloud of pixels evaporating in the air, millions of bits of colors just drifting into the sky." His panicked eyes calmed and a smile broke through. "It was awesome."

Margy laughed. Then they were laughing together. They shrieked and jumped. They screamed and spun around. They punched the air and thrust their pelvises. They took shots of Jameson.

Victor hit the button and *Adamina* lit the room. He moved OP through the streets, running at amazing speed, jumping over buildings. Margy took the controller and tripled-jumped him, sending him soaring across the atmosphere. Victor brought him back down to earth and ran him to the battered hot dog bot. The owner stared at OP cautiously.

>*fix hot dog stand*

The dents popped out. The umbrella straightened. The paint brightened. Hot dogs filled the bin.

The owner shrieked. OP hopped away.

"Should we be doing this in front of people?" Margy asked.

"OP is a god! Why not show off the power?"

"Because I don't really want creepy people making sacrifices in OP's name." She grabbed the controller out of Victor's hand. "Anyway, gods don't help people. They spy on them."

>*Sprinklesburgh County Mental Hospital*

The scene dissolved and reformed at the entrance lobby of a quiet, white facility. Nurses were sitting with patients and walking them around.

"Margy," Victor started, "this isn't a good idea. Let's just–"

>*Invisible*

OP vanished to only a faint outline. Margy moved him down the halls.

>*Wallhack*

He moved through a closed door.

An older woman sat on the small, firm bed with white sheets. She stared into the wall in front of her, rapidly mumbling incoherent words, leaving little room for breathing. Her eyes were bloodshot, as if sleep was something that had not crossed her path in a very long time.

OP left the room through a sidewall and walked through several other walls before stopping in another room. An older man sat in this one, in a chair facing the window. He didn't say a word, but his face trembled with fury. His eyes bore holes into the glass and his body shook with rage.

Margy handed the controller back to Victor and stared at the floor, eyes blank but shaking as she forced her emotions back down.

"Margy," Victor said softly, "I'm sure they're doing everything they can to help your par–"

Margy stood and left the apartment.

The zoomo Erin nodded to Margy and handed off the remote. "Everyone's out, today's specs are uploaded, I'll make sure the front door is locked behind me."

"Thanks for taking charge."

Victor gave a small wave to the passing fox as she exited.

Margy walked to the middle of the domed room and up to a large machine that sat in its center. She flipped a few switches, inserted a minidisc, and hit a red button. The machine came to life and a blue light shot from a curved lens.

She joined Victor in the reclined seats that circled the projector, its beam of light expanding to fill the dome. Stars appeared, followed by planets, and clusters, and asteroids.

Victor reached his hand up and played with a star, moving it around his reach. Margy grabbed a small planet and hit Victor's star away.

"Do you have to reset the universe every time you start it up?"

Margy shook her head. "Only if I save."

"Man, this thing is awesome. I can see why so many people want private tours." He kicked Saturn to the other side of the galaxy. "Can I touch it yet?"

"Never in your or my life will I allow you touch that machine. We only got it thanks to some guy's donation."

"It can't be that expensive."

"Try four million credits."

"Shitballs, I'll marry that guy and he won't have to worry about donating."

"Good luck," Margy said. "He doesn't swing that way."

"I'll consummate four million credits all over him and make it official."

Margy laughed. "Gross." She gently swept her hand through a star cluster, causing particles of light to run everywhere. "So, we do this. We play god."

"Which god?"

Margy shrugged. "No one writes books bashing Buddhism."

Victor leaned back even more in his chair. "We do nothing?"

"If there is a god, isn't that what it's been doing for the past billions of years? Why should we change it up?"

Victor shook his head. "Nah, I like to think a god's main priorities are who wins football games and deciding which weddings to rain out." He looked at her. "Seriously, though. If not us, it's going to be someone else. Someone worse."

Margy stared at the stars. "Okay, we do something with it. But what do we do? What in all hells do we do with OP?"

"I guess we should choose an alignment." Victor sat up. "I'm all for Batman neutral good. Going all Superman lawful good is too much work."

"Should we take a chaotic good into account? Go Wolverine on this town?"

Victor shook his head. "Wolverine adheres to strict societal rules and laws. Dude was a samurai. He's not

36

really random other than his Berserker Rage, but he works desperately to keep that in check."

"Forget good. What about a neutral? How about Deadpool?"

"He fits the bill, but I'm not cool enough for that."

Screams shattered the serene scene under the stars. Victor and Margy jumped from their comfortable chairs and ran to the lobby to find a janitor by the door, huddled in front of the glass wall overlooking the front yard of the planetarium. Victor grabbed his hair as they looked outside.

The sky was a harsh fuchsia. The grass was an oversaturated blue. The buildings, one by one, were turning all the colors of the rainbow. Giraffes roamed the streets. Clouds fell from the sky. A fifty-foot tall man strode along the river, twisting to life gigantic balloon animals that quickly ran off.

"Ah! That's OP!" Margy shrieked.

"Shit! Shitshitshitshit!" Victor yelled. "My parents!"

Margy unlocked the door and they ran out, leaving the janitor huddled in a hot mess on the floor. "What's the fastest way home?" Victor asked.

"Worm at Main and Nantucket."

Victor darted off, with Margy close behind. "I'm sure we can find a cab!"

"With all this giraffe traffic?" He dodged a balloon poodle as it lifted its leg on a tree.

"I hate wormholes! You know this!" She broke through a throng of terrified townspeople running the other way. "They're too dangerous!"

"People use them all the time." He jumped over a fallen cloud.

Margy slowed at the sight of the wormhole but Victor grabbed her and pulled her in.

There was a tug at the back of their spines and they came out the other side into their anti-universe. The colors were inverted and what was on their left was now on their right.

"Remember," Margy shook out, "do NOT touch your anti-self. It would cause both of you to cease to exist."

"Duh," Victor replied. "I was in the same safety class in elementary as you were."

They hurried through the red grass and shielded their eyes from the bright orange sky. Passers-by nodded and greeted them before going on with their business. Instead of every-car-for-itself as it was in their universe, drivers obeyed the signals. In place of kids swapping animal heads with their *Clone Me, Splice Me!*™ kits, the tikes played peacefully with sport balls, kites, and water balloons.

"This place creeps me out," Margy said.

"I still don't get it," Victor said. "Shouldn't they be running around, too? Where are their anti-giraffes?"

"They're still in the zoo. It's just anti, not a mirror world. C symmetry, not P."

"Oh, yeah, right. C." Victor looked around. "There it is," he pointed. "Hurry up, my parents can do a lot of damage in ten seconds."

Lyssa and Johnny Vance relaxed on the large foam balls in their son's apartment and Mort nestled in Johnny's lap. A pile of NineX games sat next to Lyssa, who held the NarviPlay controller.

"Why a chicken?" Johnny asked. "He's such a talented boy. Maybe he's losing his creative edge."

"We should send him on a trip," Lyssa suggested, guiding a fifty-foot OP through the streets. "This game is fun and all, but for the life of me, I can't figure out the point."

"Maybe redesign the world some more. Add more crab rangoon."

"Ooh! A Lamaze class! Let's drive through it!"

The front door flew open and Victor and Margy ran in. Mort barked and scuttled about. Victor dove over the couch and hit the controller out of his mother's hand.

"What the shit, guys!" he yelled.

"Heeeeey," his dad replied.

38

Margy grabbed the controller and opened the command center.

>*Undo all*

Victor hurried over and peeked through the blinds. "Nope. Doesn't work."

"This is going to take a while." Margy rolled her eyes. "I can't wait to see the news now."

>*Invisible*

OP vanished to a faint outline.

"Mom, Dad!" Victor shouted. "Why are you here?"

"Hey, now," Johnny said, standing. "We told you we were coming by to grab some games. Lyssa spotted a new console so we thought we'd play. It was the only game we saw for it."

"You can't do that!"

"Well, this is a new rule." Lyssa frowned.

"No, no, you *can*," Victor tried to explain, "just–"

"Victor," Margy interrupted, her fingers flying as they typed in commands, "this isn't the time."

Victor nodded. "I'll see you guys tomorrow." He motioned down the hallway and to his back door. His parents gave each other confused glances before picking up the NineX games and leaving.

"It's not going to take them long to find out what happened today and connect it all together." Margy said, sitting on the couch as she continued to turn their town back to normal. Mort barked around her, sniffing her legs. Just as Margy was about to change an M.C. Escher building back to its normal state, a green glow filled the screen.

*Hey! Listen! Listen to me!*

"W. T. Fuck." Margy growled. "It's that stupid flying orb again."

Now sitting next to her, Victor sighed, head sinking into his hands. "Ignore it, it'll go away."

"Look at all these things they changed.... The river is now chocolate a la *Willy Wonka*, so now I get to restock some marine life. There are some playgrounds where the ground literally *is* lava, so there are some terrified kids stuck on never-ending swing rides. And *why* do all the dogs now have three legs!"

"My mom has a thing for three-legged dogs."

"This will take all night."

Victor stood and Mort followed at his feet. "I'll order the flying turtle pizza."

# Chapter Five

## Portable is Betterable

Thousands of miles away, in a room that was windowless but heavy on wall decorations, thirteen men and women sat around a circular table. Television screens covered one wall. Usually these screens relayed what was happening in different parts of the world; today, however, they all focused on the small town of Sprinklesburgh, Indiana.

Tensions were high. The air was thick. They had been in this room for almost twenty-four hours. Granted, they rarely left the room, but at the moment, they had no choice but to stay.

"What do you *mean* we can't find him!" Agent One yelled.

"He—she... they—is not connected," Samus replied, her voice pushing through forced patience. "How are we supposed to find someone if they're off the grid?"

"How would he be able to download anything if he wasn't connected to the infranet in the first place!" His voice was able to get louder with each word. "I need *someone* to tell me what the hell is going on here!"

The table was quiet as everyone shuffled through their papers. One man finally stood.

"Sir and ma'am," Pit said cautiously, "this is quite a long shot but... I believe this is related to a much earlier incident... one we've seen before."

Agent One fell into his chair and Samus leaned forward. "Go on," she said.

Pit nodded. "Does anyone else remember the terrorist Tyson Brahe?"

The table erupted into interjections from all around.

"Uh... *who?*" a voice cut through, his thick, bored drawl immediately receiving annoyed glares from the members around the table.

"Fuck, Derek, don't you know anything?"

Samus let out a shrill whistle, cutting through noise. "Pit. Continue."

Pit nodded with hesitation. "It's the same... *abilities...* if you will." He walked over to the screens, directing their eyes to the fuchsia sky and blue grass. "The ability to easily manipulate the world." He pointed to a screen with the giant chicken. "Odd sightings that can't be written off as UFOs or 'scientific unexplainables'." He moved to the screen with the fifty-foot OP, warped and barely identifiable. "And *this* man—" he pulled out his remote and projected it on a large screen, "—is someone we've seen before." He used his remote to project another picture of OP. The camera barely caught him, but there was no mistake that it was the same person. "Sir, ma'am, the rest of the Panel.... We know Tyson Brahe isn't controlling him. But someone else is. And they have the same abilities that Tyson had... Which means they have the game." The room once again blew up in chaos. "If they find out the truth, they can figure out the equation."

"There's no one in the world now who could make the connection," Agent One said, quieting everyone. "Tyson was given the game by that traitor, Marie, and told to find a formula. He couldn't figure the equation out and he knew what he was looking for."

"That doesn't null the fact that this prime intellect has this—"

"A *whaaa?*" The lazy question slipped from the back of Derek's throat and splattered on the floor. Samus seethed as she controlled her fury.

"That doesn't null the fact that this prime intellect has this immense power," Samus continued. "We call this someone a *prime intellect* because he is unmatched and unstoppable if his full potential is unlocked." She glared at Derek's half-open eyes, daring him to ask another question. "This person is dangerous and we have to find him somehow."

"We wouldn't be in this mess," someone wheezed nasally, "if you guys didn't lose the game in the first place. All you had to do was capture Tyson and lock up the game. That was all. But nooooooo…" He jiggled as he moved his head in an exaggerated circle. "Let's pass the game person to person to try and hack and deconstruct it. Oh? Someone can't remember where they put it?" He snorted. "My, my. What are the odds?"

The red anger in Samus's face and fiery tension in her body disappeared as she seemed to relax into a state of unbelievably calm fury. Agent One quickly stepped in.

"All in favor of disposing of this prime intellect," he proposed.

"Aye," everyone responded.

"*How?*" Samus asked.

"There's only one way," Pit said. "And that's the internet."

"We've already been over this," Samus started, "he's not connected–"

"-to the in*fra*net," Pit interrupted. "I'm talking about THE INTERNET. It was what we all were running on so long ago. I'm not surprised many don't remember."

"I remember," Derek's mumbling voice said with pride. Samus threw a stapler at him.

"The old internet—" Pit went on, "—was a sluggish, hellish terrain of airwaves and binary numbers. We cast it aside and locked it off in order to create the new infranet. As you know, while we're always connected to the infranet, particularly physically, the *internet* was just an outside search engine for posting cat photos and watching porn. The worst parts of humanity are locked in it."

"What does this have to do with our current problem?" someone yawned.

"It's the only way we're going to find this new terrorist," Pit answered. "They have the game we lost so many years ago, which only runs on the airwave and binary number system...." Pit straightened. "We have to connect to the old internet."

The room erupted in mayhem.

"Are you *insane*?"

"That will unleash chaos!"

"We locked that place away for a reason!"

"We'd be doing more harm than good!"

"SILENCE!"

The room froze as Samus glared them all down.

"Entropy has begun," Agent One said, "and the longer we leave it, the more disordered everything will get. We don't have a choice. We'll just need to be ready for clean-up."

The room was quiet. All had turned several shades paler, except Derek, who replied with a lazy smile.

"Pit," Samus said. "Connect your search team."

Margy bit into her sandwich. "Do you ever wake up with the taste of blood in your mouth?"

Victor stopped mid-bite. "No?" He eyed her. "Another episode?"

Margy didn't say anything. The two went back to eating at the small cafe on Main Street, enjoying the sunny day on the outside terrace. A homeless man shuffled past, stopped, and looked at Victor's meal.

"That's an inappropriate lunch," he said, before moving on.

Victor shoved the last two bites of the Bacon Goliath into his mouth.

"When homeless people are commenting on your food choices," Margy said, "you've hit rock bottom."

"UGH!" Victor put his head on the table. "Stinky Stan is right. That meal was entirely too much." He grabbed his stomach. "Oh, Zeus, I feel the stunning pangs of regret."

"All up in your poo hole?"

"No, much higher up, though I'm sure it will slide south." Victor whimpered. "Six strips of bacon. Six strips of flying-turtle bacon. Four slabs of beef. Four slices of processed cheese. Three buns.... It doesn't *sound* like a lot."

"Are you fucking serious? That IS a lot! I warned you as you were ordering it!"

Victor squirmed and tears came to his eyes. "My body is rejecting this like a diseased kidney. Hoooooo hee hee hooooooo. Oh, you were right, Margy, you were right. I shouldn't've gotten it. It was too much!"

"It was too much when you said the first six strips of bacon."

"Plus fries."

"Gods, man! Why don't you just send starving kids in Africa a picture of you pissing on a buffet table?" She went back to eating.

"That reminds me..." Victor breathed out. "I have a funny story to tell you once you finish your calamari."

Margy moved the fried squid away from her mouth and instead looked to the street. It was a peaceful day with fewer people out and about, most likely due to the incidents of the past two days. But those who were out in the sun were enjoying it. That was, until someone screamed.

"What now?" Victor gurgled, pulling his head off the table.

Three wolves came charging down the street. They stopped in front of Victor and Margy, howled at the moon, and continued to run. They ran a bit further down the street, stopped, and again howled at the moon.

"That... doesn't happen every day," Victor mumbled.

An unusually tall man with a slender frame slowly made his way down the sidewalk. The suit he wore was skin-tight. A small, green man with bulging eyes dotted with red pupils smiled maniacally while he held up his long, twisted fingers to people as they ran away. A deformed man shaped as a banana ran down the street swinging a katana. He stopped and shouted a battle cry into the air.

"IT'S CASHEW MARGARINE JAM TIME!" he said, slicing his blade through a mailbox.

"Huh," Victor said, "that's not right at all."

"What is going on?" Margy asked, unable to stop staring at the stream of nonsense filling the street, which

45

was now being overrun by turtles, foxes, and hedgehogs. A squirrel popped into view on the cafe railing.

"Come on," Victor said, "we've got to stop this."

They ran down the street and back to Victor's place. Mort barked as they entered the apartment. As Victor turned on *Adamina*, Margy stared out the window.

"We're going to have to mobilize this. There's too many of them out there."

"Do you still have your handheld Opus?" Victor asked. "The jailbroken one? It would work."

As Margy ran across the street to her place, avoiding a purple and pink unicorn sticking its horns into car doors, Victor pulled up the game's map. The floating orb immediately popped into view.

*Listen! Hey! Listen to me!*

"Holy shit SHUT THE FUCK UP!" Victor yelled, clicking away. The green orb disappeared. He navigated through the map and OP appeared in front of a toy store.

Victor stared in awe. "All of my childhood dreams are coming true."

OP ran down the aisles of action figures and toy guns.

Portable Opus in hand, Margy ran out her door, only to nearly be trampled by a giant man with a long, purple cape. Under a mop of green hair that defied gravity, half of his pallid green face was hidden behind a metallic mask that covered one eye.

Margy's jaw dropped. "No fucking way...."

As she watched the giant move toward the city, there was an explosion that shook the ground. An object in the sky flew quickly upward and into the clouds.

"Victor! No!"

She ran across the street and through Victor's door.

"What are you doing!" she yelled.

"It was only a matter of time before Japanese mecha fighting got involved," Victor replied, watching the screen intently. "But it's not just *any* mecha, Margy, oh no. I've created..." Victor moved the view to make OP full screen. *"School Girl Mecha! She fights for love! She fights with flair! She fights in a metallic schoolgirl mini skirt!"*

"We don't have time for this!" Margy shrieked. "CATS is out there! You're bringing fire to fight fire, Mr. I-Don't-Want-To-Hurt-Anyone!"

"Cats aren't a threat. What a silly thing–"

"Freakin' ALL YOUR BASE CATS!"

Victor finally turned to her. "No shit?" He smiled. "Awesome."

"Park OP in invisible. We have to get out there."

Victor switched OP's opacity, parked him, and Margy ejected *Adamina* from the NarviPlay. They ran out the door with Mort at their feet.

"There he is, Agent One!" Pit shouted above the commotion in the windowless room. A large monitor zeroed in on the mecha schoolgirl rising into the clouds.

"Does your search team have an IP yet for location of connection?"

"No. It's going in and out. It's like the game doesn't even need the internet to play."

"Keep searching," Samus said. "We have to close off the old internet as soon as we can. Who knows what else is going to get through?" She turned to the rest in the room. "How's clean-up coming?"

"No fatalities yet, ma'am."

"Keep it that way!"

"Um... ma'am..." Pit gulped. He pointed to the large screen. The mecha schoolgirl and giant CATS were now head to head, grappling in the river.

"Let's MOVE, people!" Agent One yelled. "We need to lock that portal NOW!"

"We found him!"

Samus grabbed the coordinates. "Lock it up!"

Victor and Margy sat on the planetarium roof overlooking the river. Margy looked through binoculars and scanned the area while Victor battled on the portable Opus. Mort pecked the roof around them.

"Have you tried the command center and just deleting CATS?" Margy asked.

"Yeup, and several variations. It's a video game, so I guess being forced to battle makes sense."

"Don't you have a weapon?"

"I have a kick-ass vaporizer gun I'd love to use if only this little bitch would stop pulling my hair and let me grab it."

"Well, pick up the pace," Margy said, binoculars to the ground, "idiots are gathering."

"Look at this guy, he's mostly taint. I have no idea why he's so difficult to beat."

The giant schoolgirl pushed CATS back, flailed her arms around in a dramatic final move, and whipped out her gun.

*Watashi o aisuruuuu!*

A bright light burst from her gun, sending CATS flying backwards over the river, and her skirt blew upwards for a great fan service shot. Just before CATS hit the water, he froze there, hovering in the air. Then, just as the giant chicken did, he began to evaporate, pixel by pixel floating into the sky, disappearing.

*Ai no mofu, ganbatte!*

The schoolgirl blew a kiss with her two fingers, flipped them into the peace sign, and vanished.

"BOOM!" Victor punched the air. "I'm a real-life superhero! Margy, I should throw a party! I love throwing parties. I have the best parties because I have so many hats."

"You don't get that hero title until we finish cleaning up this other mess. So shed that sailor dress and get moving."

OP ran down the streets, shoving flying turtles, foxes, and hedgehogs into cages that Victor had created in the command center. Using quick punches, he sent the tall, slender gentleman and the short, green man into pixelated puffs of smoke. The banana man gave him a bit more trouble with his sword, but he was eventually obliterated.

Victor—game in hand—and Margy walked the streets, checking yards and alleys for anything out of place.

"Mort, detect," Victor commanded. The 8-bit chicken went into search mode: sniffing, flying into the sky for an aerial view, and occasionally standing completely still as his beady eyes slowly scanned the area as if he were able to see right through the walls. With Mort's help, more oddities were found and taken care of. A rabid rabbit was detained, a white, egg-shaped robot was dismantled, and a zombie was shot in the head. The sun was setting by the time Mort concluded his search.

"Check the world map," Margy said. "Anything?"

Victor scrolled through the town on the small screen. "Nope. I reckon we cleaned up this here town something fierce, little lady."

They high-fived. Victor slid the game into his back pocket and they turned onto their block.

Red and blue lights filled the street. Police cars blocked the road. As they neared, bulls dragged two people out of their apartment and slammed them onto the hood of a car.

"Shit," Victor breathed out.

"Ssssshhhhh."

Bulls ran in and out of Victor's apartment, carrying his games and systems.

"Where is he?" a bull yelled into Johnny Vance's face.

"We haven't seen him for a week," Lyssa squeaked out, flinching at the cuffs slapped onto her wrists. Her eyes flicked over and saw Victor and Margy walking on the opposite sidewalk. "He said something about visiting friends in North Dakota."

The bull snarled. "You don't find that weird? North Dakota's full of nothing but freak cults."

Margy and Victor turned toward her door.

"HEY!"

They jumped at the explosion of a voice and nearly fell backwards at the sight of a bull charging them.

"What do you know about the kid that lives there?" the bull thundered, pinning them against the facade of her apartment. Mort barked at his feet, pecking his ankles.

"Never saw him," Margy answered easily. "Dork liked too many video games to ever come out."

"Is that so?" the bull looked at Victor. "And who are you?"

"Well," Margy answered, "hopefully my fuck buddy for tonight, if you haven't made him go into complete hiding."

The bull let them go, shaking off the chicken that had clasped onto his boot. "Kids these days."

As he made his way back across the street, Victor and Margy headed into her apartment, locking the door behind them.

"Blech," Victor scrunched his face. "It smells like IKEA in here. Like boxed furniture and meatballs."

"Get used to it. You'll be here for a while."

# Chapter Six

## Down the Dodgy Rabbit Hole

The various news apps that lit Margy's wall were calming down. Happenings in the little town of Sprinklesburgh had given its residents something to talk about for a few days before they got on with their regular business. Margy and Victor left *Adamina* off but kept the handheld game in their possession at all times, swapping off when they went to work.

"So, you're going with super secret government conspiracy?" Margy asked into the phone speaker, unimpressed. In the dark domed room at the planetarium, she put the planets and stars back in order for the next showing.

Victor sat in his cube, his phone screen showing Margy not taking him the least bit seriously. "It's *always* a super secret government conspiracy!" he insisted, designing a familiar ordered by a little girl. Despite her *~SuGaRfAiRyPrInCeSs~* screen name, the familiar was requested to be a hand-sized version of a tardigrade. After a quick image search, Victor decided to give her waterbear bug familiar a couple of extra perks for being so damn awesome.

"Fine," Margy sighed, "explain it."

"Where did all of that stuff come from? The animals, the people, the things?"

"Last time it was your parents and their sick sense of humor."

"But it wasn't *this* time," Victor said. "And it wasn't us. Did you notice they were all coming from the same direction?"

51

Margy stopped. "No. You noticed something like that?"

"Kind of hard not to. *Now*. Why were there police at my place?"

"So many responses to that."

"Shut up. They had my games. *Obviously* they were looking for *Adamina*. But how did they know *I* had it?"

"Okay. So, the raiding of your place is linked to *Adamina*," Margy said. "But how was that mess of outdated memes related to us?"

"How does someone as smart as you not clearly see it was a trap?"

Margy was silent. She hated it when Victor solved puzzles before she did.

"Obviously the government opened the Ark of the Covenant again," Victor said. "All hell broke loose, Nazi faces melted off, and they created mayhem—this time to draw OP out into public."

"Which you more than did."

"Shut up. Once OP was out in public, they knew they had our attention, that we were playing. And then it's easy to find us through our connection."

"But we're never connected to the infranet when we play," Margy said. "The news boxes tell us we have to connect."

Now Victor was quiet. "That's what confuses me. They had to do something on their end to find us. They took a risk with those monsters."

Another tour group made their way into the domed room. "Look, I have to go. Let's chat more tonight at home."

"Gross." Victor shivered. "Don't ever again sound so domesticated with me."

The administration room was thick with tension. Samus and Agent One glared at each member around the circular table, who hung their heads, avoiding eye contact.

"We know Victor's name," Samus pressed out, "his address. His IP. The off-brand toothpaste he uses. But we can't find him?"

The room was quiet for several moments with no one wanting to speak up.

"He's... just a drone," Pit finally shook out. "We can't search for something that barely exists."

"Then that means..." Agent One said, "he's not alone. Someone, an *actual* someone, is helping him. *That* or a meta since they're the only ones capable of irregular thought!"

The table went up in "Ohhhhhhh"s.

"So, like, what's the diffy there?" Derek asked, raising his hand. "Drone... meta..."

Agent One glared and Samus pursed her lips, leaving Pit to explain. "A drone is unbought, unaltered. They have a specific line of programming to follow. A *bought* drone, however—a *meta*—is one being prepped for use and takeover. Its line of programming has obviously been altered, and therefore, can have irregular thoughts. They're the people on the street corner shouting nonsense through a megaphone. They're the people asking questions that shouldn't be answered. *They're* the people who are going too deep in manipulating life and nature."

"Like, scientists?" Derek smiled, proud of himself for figuring it out. Samus's glare refused to acknowledge him.

"The more these people dig," Agent One added, "the better chance they have at figuring out the truth. Some already have but are passed off as lunatics. And why? Why do people brush aside their rants?" He looked at the blank-faced members sitting around the table waiting for an answer. "Because they don't have the equation to back up what they're spouting."

The table again went up in "Ohhhhhhh"s.

"God DAMN IT!" Samus yelled. "What are you people hired for? Did you get this job because you won some crap online contest?"

"I did, ma'am," Derek said, his slow twang slithering through.

"Will someone GET HIM OUT OF HERE!" Samus screamed. "The rest of you, search for his accomplice! The safety of this world is at stake!"

Margy paced her kitchen area, Victor sat in the birthing position on the floor, working on his breathing, and Mort pecked at the wall. Margy's apartment was far less inviting than Victor's, which was the feng shui she was going for.

"I will bet you a thousand credits," Victor said, "hee hee hoooo... that they can't find *Adamina* without doing whatever it was they did that released those other creatures."

"And what makes you think they won't?" Margy asked.

"They're not going to take that risk again. They only did it to—hee hee hoooo—find us, and we weren't there."

"What in all hells do we do? Continuing to assume they aren't going to find *us* is asinine."

"Hooooo... Yeah..." Victor nodded. "We should probably leave."

"And what? Live a life on the run?"

Victor halted mid-exhale and racked his brain for an idea. After several moments of nothing, he continued his exercises. "Meh. That's Future Victor's problem."

Margy shook her head and went to the fridge, defeated. "Future Victor must hate you for everything you put on him."

Victor shrugged. "I don't know anything about that guy. What I *do* know is, Past Victor is an asshole."

Margy plopped on her couch and Mort hopped on her lap. "We have the power of the world in our hands. We have to be able to figure this out." She grabbed the Opus off the armrest and passed it Victor. "There has to be some sort of mission on here. An Easter egg. *Something.*"

Victor looked at Margy as he took the game. "Are you sure?"

"Do it, bitch."

He pressed the power button and OP appeared on screen. "Now what?"

*Hey! Listen to me! Hey!*

"This thing will never go away, will it?" Victor seethed.
"Just listen to it to shut it up."
Victor rolled his eyes and accepted the conversation.

> *The fate of the world is in*
> *your hands! You are*
> *running blind. Follow me!*

Victor turned OP away.
"Follow it, asshat."
Victor grunted, set OP to invisible, and followed the glowing green orb for an hour, going down the streets of Sprinklesburgh, along the river, and across several soybean fields.
"Isn't there a fast travel?" Victor groaned.
OP ran down a long, gravel road hidden by a cornfield. Then another, and another. He breached the edge of the woods and continued in. Victor handed the controller up to Margy.
"An hour and a half. My thumb needs a break."
Margy opened the command center.

> *>Free run*

OP's MPH increased tenfold and he was speeding through the forest behind the buzzing orb with wings.
"Thanks for the tip!" he muttered sarcastically.
"That's what she said."
Minutes later, the green orb stopped cold. OP stood in front of a large mound.
"Are... they on the Native American historical grounds? This looks like one of their hills."
"We've been there three times for field trips," Margy said. "We've never seen this one."

> *Hey! Hey! Follow me!*

The green orb floated around to the other side and zipped through a brush-covered hidden doorway into the mound.

The glowing familiar lit the space to reveal a tomb. Several decorated skeletons laid peacefully around a center hole that dropped deep into the earth.

*Hurry! Through here!*

"Awesome," Victor smiled. "Super secret bonus level!"

The familiar disappeared into the darkness. Margy pushed OP in.

He vanished.

The screen continued to look into the dark hole.

"What happened to OP?" Margy asked.

"Oh, sweet gods, we killed him!"

"What do we do!"

"Restart! Restart!"

Margy turned the game off and back on. The screen started up right where they left off—staring into the bottomless pit where they had just sent OP.

"BREAK IT DOWN!"

Victor and Margy jumped at the shout right outside her apartment. A moment later there was a loud bang as something heavy hit her door. Margy ran toward the back porch and peered out the window; bulls had surrounded the place.

"What do we do?" Victor shrieked.

Margy picked up the game.

>*413 E Middle St, Sprinklesburgh, IN*
>*Trap door in closet*
>*Trap door leads to playground*

"Like that's going to work!" Victor yelled under his breath.

"It's all we have!" Margy pulled Victor to the closet with Mort at their feet. The front door gave in and they heard several bulls running into the place.

"We're fucked! We're so fucked!"

Moments later, a bull ripped open the closet door and Victor and Margy screamed.

The bull grabbed them.

At least, he tried to.

All three looked down to the bull's furry hands grasping onto nothing, and Victor and Margy's legs and stomachs evaporated into a cloud of pixels that quickly moved up their torsos. Victor shrieked.

The bull's face filled with horrified fury as he tried again and again to grasp them, but shortly later, the two disappeared from the closet completely.

Pixel by pixel, Margy and Victor came back together in the abandoned playground full of wormholes and portals. They looked around, their breaths shaking as the moon gleamed back at them.

Victor laughed. "It worked! Margy, you're a genius!"

A swirling of light appeared next to them and a pair of bull hooves appeared on the concrete.

"Ah! Margy, you moron! Turn it off!"

Margy's fingers fumbled with the Opus as more of the bull appeared.

>*Seal trap door*

The light faded. Now, in the middle of the playground, a pair of bull legs in police pants kicked, stuck where they had appeared.

"I feel bad for the kid who discovers that."

"Screw the kid," Margy said. "I now have half a bull stuck in my closet."

They looked around them. The evening was quiet and the streets were nearly deserted. Mort pecked at the ground, cautiously venturing only a few feet away.

"Where are we going to go now?" Victor asked.

Margy pulled the game back up, the screen still showing the deep pit. "The same place OP went."

They ran down the streets of Sprinklesburgh, following the river. They ran across the same soybean fields with the sound of crickets muffling the noise of their run. Mort glided above them, his two-dimensional body waning in and out of sight depending on the angle he flew. They came upon the long, gravel road hidden by the cornfield, where they nearly collapsed from exhaustion.

"Behind... the silo there..." Victor panted out. "Shirley Hardy... It's where I got... my first boner...."

Margy gave him an incredulous look before continuing. They went down another gravel road, and another, surrounded by corn.

"I'm in my worst nightmares," Margy muttered.

"Being chased by the government?"

"No, being stuck in a maze of corn forever."

Victor chuckled. "*Maize* of corn...."

The moon moved higher into the sky as Jupiter lowered. The edge of the woods finally came into view.

"Damn... boondocks..." Margy panted. "Not a wormhole in sight...."

"You wouldn't take one anyway."

"Shut up."

The trees thickened and their surroundings dimmed. Mort landed softly, then strutted beside them. The dull roar of chirping crickets drowned out all other noise. Finally, the mound appeared through the trees, outlined by the moonlight. They ran their hands along the outer edge, looking for the opening, until Victor fell into it.

"Oof!... Found it."

Inside the hill was a damp coolness, and a darkness that wouldn't let up. They pulled out their remotes and clicked on their flashlights. The glow revealed the decorated skeletons in ceremonial garb, just as OP had discovered them.

Margy pointed her flashlight to the low ceilings that showed no sign of archeological examination. "I think this place only pops up with God Mode activated. Look at this, nothing's been touched. Like, ever."

"Why here?" Victor asked. "What's so special about a place every fourth grader in the tri-state area visits?"

She shrugged as they moved toward the center. "They were the first people in the area? It's the most rooted place in Sprinklesburgh's history? There's nothing special whatsoever about this?"

They stepped to the edge of the deep pit in the center and pointed their lights into the void.

"No bottom."

"Wormhole?" Victor asked.

Margy shook her head "My money's on portal. If it were a wormhole it would always be here, God Mode or not."

Victor swallowed as the darkness swallowed their light. "Do we have the balls to do this?"

"I don't know. There are more bad outcomes than favorable... so, going by the law of probability, this won't turn out well."

Victor looked down at Mort, who was waiting right next to him. He took a breath and held out his hand. "Shall we?"

Margy placed her hand in Victor's.

They stepped over the edge.

# Chapter Seven

## The Reappearance of Tyson Brahe

There were only a few moments when the air whipped around them as they fell. Margy held her breath, Victor let a shriek escape him, and Mort growled. Then gravity shifted and they found themselves gently drifting downward.

"Is that still you, Victor?"

"Hee hee hoooooo... Hee hee hoooooo...."

"Good."

A faint light appeared under them, revealing that they had been slowly descending past hovering objects that stayed stationary throughout their fall. A dancing baby came into view and continued to dance as they fell past it. Signs with broken English read "THROW MISCHIEVOUS COOK HABITUALLY DRUNK THE SEA" and:

ALL OF YOU LISTEN TO MEE, DON'T DISTURB
HERE, I WILL CALL POLICE CATCH YOU, I HATE
ALL OF YOU.

A subdued bear floated, an army sergeant munched on a pork chop sandwich, and a king penguin waddled about with a penguin backpack wrapped around his flippers.

A checkered floor appeared below them and just as they were stretching to place their feet, the gravity kicked to full, and they slammed into the linoleum face first. Mort barked angrily.

Pushing themselves to their feet, a plain black door with the number 10 on it loomed in front of them. Looking up, the ceiling disappeared into darkness and empty walls offered no other exit. Victor nodded to Margy and she turned the knob.

The sun momentarily blinded them as they stepped outside. A vast, empty desert stretched before them with monoliths and sand dunes dotting the dusty plains. An old, Wild West town sat nearby with people and... *things* making their way up and down the street. Victor and Margy looked at each other, nodded, and stepped toward the town.

"We either took some bad drugs," Margy said, "we're dead, or something much more improbable happened which my brain can't wrap around just yet."

"This is happening, Margy," Victor said, "and the sooner you accept it, the sooner you can figure out how to get us out of here."

"Things like this don't just happen, Victor!" Margy shrieked. "All of science is to prove that nothing *just happens*, but that everything is following a fundamental order. That's basic Hawking 101! All of this—OP, mecha schoolgirl, this place—it's all impossible! And the only solution I have is just... too messed up."

"Tie up your nervous breakdown and get moving. We're bound to get some answers here."

The three stepped into the town and tumbleweeds bounced across the dirt road. A dark mass moved across the horizon, followed by a low murmur of purrs.

"That..." Victor squinted his eyes, "is a herd of cats."

"A massive herd of cats...."

Their cat gazing was interrupted when a group of small, fat, boiled-over dwarves trudged past them.

"Hey fagot wut got on ur face."

"Mayb u shldnt have votred for tht asshol."

"TROLOLOfu."

Victor tightened his fists. "The fu–"

Margy grabbed his shoulder and pointed to a sign on a nearby shop.

*DO NOT FEED THE TROLLS*

"Ya bitch let ur grlfrend tell u wut tod o."

"Pussybitch."

"Winey bleedingheart libs."

Victor and Mary turned away and continued into town. "I'll cunt punt them to China, assholes," Victor growled.

"Come on, douche." Margy pulled them into the first inviting shopfront she saw. They went through the double swinging doors and stopped cold.

A woman was floating in the air with tentacles hovering around her, which slowly wrapped around each of her limbs. The patrons of the saloon cheered as she enjoyed every moment of it.

"Yeah," Margy breathed out. "I've seen enough hentai to know where this is going."

She pulled Victor out and they continued down the street.

"You suck," Victor mumbled. "Japanese porn is the best."

"I already can't eat scrambled eggs because of a god damned Japanese video I once saw. I'd hate to cut out seafood as well."

"Rule 34, Margy. You just haven't seen it yet."

Shocked owls, rabbits with pancakes on their heads, and smarmy sloths moved about the town, keeping Mort close to Victor's feet. A honey badger tore open a snake with its fangs. Victor chuckled.

"I love that one."

Margy peeked into another saloon before fully entering. Inside was a normal-looking bar with some drinkers scattered about.

"Hey, guys!" the bartender called to them, smiling. "Welcome, welcome! Come on and sit and I'll grab you something to enjoy!"

Victor and Margy took stools next to a man hunched over his glass while the bartender set two drinks down in front of them.

"My name's Greg, and if you need anything, just let me know." He smiled again and went back to cleaning the bar.

"Great idea, Margy," Victor said. "Let's get shitfaced before we try to save the world."

"We're only trying to save ourselves."

"How did you two get in here?" a gruff voice asked, causing the two to swivel their seats. Glaring at them was a man in his forties, donning a five o'clock shadow over his strong jaw, with a cowboy hat sitting on a full matte of dark hair. An unbuttoned flannel shirt rested over a dusty white t-shirt, and a simple leather belt was buckled over a rough pair of dark jeans. His eyes were tired but still a striking shade of blue.

"I said, how did you get in here?"

"You could say we fell down the rabbit hole," Margy said cautiously.

"It looked more like a pit for bodies," Victor added.

"You came here yourselves?" Victor and Margy nodded. "Why would you do that?"

"Why not?" Margy asked.

"This is the old internet. You fools are stuck here now."

Victor and Margy looked around the bar and at the old memes that were sucking on bottles until they were dry. A young guy in a brown hat that was tilted to the side gave them the finger. The two went slightly pale.

"I'm afraid I didn't understand you, sir," Victor said, turning back. "But it sounded like you said we're *stuck* in the infranet."

"Internet, not infranet. And yeup." He took a drink. "Welcome to hell."

They stared at the man, searching him for answers. "You'll have to be blunt with us," Margy said. "We're new to the area."

The man motioned for another drink. "How long have you had the game?"

Victor and Margy looked at each other, fidgeting.

"A...bout a week," Margy said. "But how–"

"And you still haven't figured out what's happening? What you are? Where you're from?" The man laughed. "That equation's never gonna be solved."

Margy let out a groan of annoyance. "What equation, *sir*?"

"Brahe. Tyson Brahe."

"What kind of name is that?" Victor asked.

"My creator had a thing for the stars."

Victor looked at Margy. "Your... mom?"

"You could call her that," Tyson shrugged. "Creator is far more apt."

Margy sat taller. "Your creator was a she?"

"My creator, your creator, your world's creator. Before she died, Marie coded me with all the math and science knowledge she could enter. She hoped I'd be able to solve the equation on my own after finding out the truth. But there wasn't enough time, and seventy-three years ago, with the last of her strength, she put me in the game." He took a drink, his hand tightening around his glass. "She created *it all* and they wouldn't even let her use it, not even at the end of her life. That was her—" he quoted with his fingers, "—reward... for feeling compassion for the drones." Tyson's anger quickly subsided with a sigh and he chuckled into his glass. "She tried to set them, you all... us... free."

Margy looked at him, soaking in every word she heard, trying to piece it all together. Victor, however, stood and stepped away. "Sorry, man, I'm just—I'm not grasping something here. Could you—"

"You heard me correctly, kid. There is no Santa Claus." He stopped mid-drink and an amused grin appeared. "There could be, if you wanted, actually. You have the power."

Margy continued to stare calmly, albeit somewhat tensely, while it was Victor's turn to break down. "Power? *Power*? What fucking power? What the—"

"The code, kid!" Tyson slammed his fist on the bar. "The disc with the cheat on it. You have it, or else you wouldn't be here. Or else you'd be sitting at home continuing with your mundane life doing nothing of significance. Just like most of those dead shells out there."

Margy inhaled deeply, the stale air and grains of sand scratching her esophagus. "You need to elucidate, Mr. Brahe."

There was a clink as Tyson set his glass down. His chair squeaked as he turned to Margy. His blue eyes captivated her.

"cmV2ZWFsIGhpc3Rvcnk="

The letters and numbers rushed out of his mouth in a brief exhalation. A blue screen popped between the two, covered in coding. Tyson's eyes scanned the lines of letters and numbers. Margy watched as he scrolled through, absorbing it all. Finally, his eyes moved back to her.

"You... already know what's going on?" Tyson asked, almost surprised. Margy looked away, her eyes hardening. "This coding about your parents and how you're helping them in the asylum..." He looked back at the screen. "Your reactions to when you reappear from your blackouts..." He scrolled further down, mumbling, "How you play *Adamina* and work with OP is how one would play if..." He shook his head. "Y2xvc2U="

The screen disappeared and Tyson's full attention was on Margy.

"I'm right, aren't I? You know what's happening. Why are you acting oblivious? Why are you leaving him in the dark?" He motioned to Victor and his voice rasped with anger. "Why haven't you moved in on the Panel? Do you realize how little time you have?"

She gulped and shook her head. "I *don't* know what's happening. The only explanation... idea... I have is *just* not possible."

"Not possible or unacceptable?" Tyson asked. Margy didn't answer. "Look at where you are. How you got here. What you've seen. Things *are* impossible. There's a reason for every impossibility. You know what that reason is, and I'm confirming that it's true."

Her breath escaped her and her shoulders sunk. Her defeated eyes dropped to the floor.

"What's true, Margy?" Victor squeaked, growing paler by the second. "What's going on?" Sensing his owner's disturbance, Mort's 8-bit feathers rustled.

Margy broke away from Tyson and turned to Victor, unable to look him in the eye. "We're... we're not–"

The saloon violently shook and the roof began to crumble. Wood and sand rained down upon them. A large beam cracked, splintered, and dropped, and Tyson pushed them to the side as it fell. They ran with the other memes to the road and watched as the bar crumbled under the claws of a several-legged, several-armed creature that was covered in spikes, bright red, and flickering green and blue bolts of electricity. Its massive size blocked out the descending sun, giving it a fiery halo. Margy and Victor stood frozen in place as its shadow engulfed them. Mort barked at their feet.

# Chapter Eight

## All Your Base

Margy's wide eyes looked to Tyson for an explanation.

"Don't tell me you've never seen a computer virus before!" He grabbed her wrist and pulled her away as the virus lunged for them.

"How do you kill something like that?" Victor yelled, running behind them, dodging screaming people. Above him, Mort flapped his pixelated wings as fast as he could.

"Come on, Margy," Tyson yelled back. "Don't go all damsel in distress on me. You know what's happening, you know how to stop it!"

"I'm only at hypothesis!" Margy panted. "I haven't had time for theory!"

"This is enough to jump straight to conclusion!"

He let go of her wrist and continued running.

Margy whipped around to Victor. "Keep running!" She grabbed the handheld Opus from his back pocket and ran toward the virus.

"Margy!" As Victor tried to run after her, Tyson grabbed him and bolted the other way.

"What are you doing?" Victor yelled. "Help her!"

"I am!"

With the virus charging toward her, Margy came to a halt and powered on the Opus. The screen lit up and showed her perplexed, scared face. She looked up to find OP standing before her. He was normal, an everyman with average looks. Calm, waiting for an order. There was almost a hint of relief in his eyes as if he were happy to see her.

A giant claw came down and squashed him like a bug.

Margy screamed and ran, the virus close behind. She could feel the prickling of electricity in the air as it moved in closer. Her hands fumbled with the Opus. She heard Victor yelling in the background. The ground shook. The Opus dropped from her hands but she couldn't stop running with the virus so close. From the corner of her eye, she could see Tyson loading a shotgun and sprinting to catch up.

"Shit. She's not doing it!" Tyson yelled.

"What should she be doing?" Victor asked. "Damn it! Help her!"

The ground shook again and Margy tumbled to the dirt. The monstrous virus hovered over her.

"Help her faster!" Victor shouted.

She flipped onto her back and shrieked as a claw flew down.

"TWFyZ3kgbGltYm8=" Tyson shouted, which echoed over the dusty plains. Margy uncovered her eyes to see a claw sticking straight through her abdomen.

Yet she felt nothing.

In place of guts and gore, her body was quickly dissipating. She looked to Victor and Tyson, but everything went dark before she could focus.

And then she was gone.

Usually the exploding of a shotgun two feet away from Victor's ear would have startled him, but instead he stared horrified at the empty space where Margy had lain. The virus moved around on its several legs, trying to find a target that seemed to have disappeared into thin air, leaving behind nothing but a puff of sand and pixels.

Victor gaped in disbelief. "She's gone."

Another blast of the shotgun echoed along the desert.

The virus turned and ran toward Victor and Tyson, its several legs shaking. Victor moved to run but Tyson held him there. The virus was closing in on them, wobbling, swaying. Victor again tried to move, but Tyson stood his ground, confident in his two shots. The pointed creature fell to the dirt, the momentum of its weight pushing it forward.

"Miscalculated. Run away!" Tyson dove to the side and Victor scrambled just in time. The virus slid past them and finally came to a halt. It laid there, flickering as its power weakened.

"Where is she?" Victor jumped up. "Where is she!"

He tackled Tyson to the ground and tried punching him, but Tyson easily grabbed Victor's arms and pulled them behind his back.

"ZnJlZXpl," Tyson said.

Victor froze. His limbs were stuck in a catatonic state.

Tyson stood and dusted himself off. "You drones are easy when you've been taking down viruses for the past several decades." He pulled out a set of binoculars and scanned the horizon. "Your friend is losing herself and you can't help. You can't even help yourself." He focused the lenses. "Right there. That's where she'll come back. It shouldn't be long. dW5sb2Nr." Victor's body went limp and he fell to the ground. Tyson grabbed Victor's collar and pulled him up, dragging him along as he tried to find his feet again.

"What—what the fuck..." Victor gasped. "How did–"

"I'm not much into exposition," Tyson interrupted. "Just wait for Margy to return."

The two continued on toward the sunset while the heat rippled off the ground. A random cat occasionally poked out from behind a rock before going back into hiding. Long after the red sun set and the colors in the dry sky disappeared, Tyson stopped near a large rock and began to set up camp. They gathered wood and Tyson created a small fire while the stars popped out one by one. He reloaded his shotgun with a couple of syringes full of a black liquid.

"Huh..." He scanned the dark horizon. "Wonder what's taking so long."

"Mort!" Victor yelled into the vast expanse. "Mooooooort!" Victor retraced their steps for several hundred feet but came running back. "I don't see chicken feet in the dirt at all. I don't know where we lost him." He turned back to the horizon. "MOOOOOOORT!"

"He's probably cat food now," Tyson responded, balling up his jacket and putting it between a rock and his back. Victor's jaw tensed and he looked to the darkened sky.

"Why isn't she back yet?" Victor asked, still looking. Only the dark sky stared back.

Several hours after getting comfortable against the rocks, a low vibration rattled the pebbles around them. It grew stronger and louder, causing the cats in the area to whine in annoyance. The vibration grew until Victor felt as if he'd be sick and it finally stopped when Margy appeared out of thin air, standing on her two feet but falling to the ground. She was now in a high school blue and gold cheerleader outfit, complete with a small slitted skirt and white tennis shoes. A white headband pulled her short hair back, with some locks temporarily dyed in matching blue and gold colors. Glitter sparkled on her eyes.

She keeled over and vomited.

"Welcome back from oblivion," Tyson smiled. "I see you took a detour on your way back here."

Margy wiped her mouth. "Why do I feel so god damned drunk?"

"Looks like you just came back from homecoming," Tyson said, handing a flask of water to Margy, who chugged it. "Also looks like your buyer can't decide how she wants you. Do you often come back dressed differently?"

Margy nodded her wobbling head. "So, that explains that, *I guess.*"

Victor let out a shriek that was half annoyance, half horrified confusion. He jumped to his feet. "WHAT. Is going ON?" He desperately looked back and forth at the two: Tyson had an amused grin that he was trying to hide and Margy was too exhausted to say anything. "I'm okay with OP somehow existing—and, by the way, we should probably check on him—and for some reason I was okay with somehow magically arriving in the Old West. But shit got REAL and I don't know what REAL is anymore!"

"Exactly. What is *real?*" Tyson asked, his eyes moving to the stars. "We believe we're more real than the games our world created. So those who created us should be even more real than we are. Everything's subjective."

"SHUT IT!" Victor shouted. Margy gave him a worried look and Tyson pulled out a second flask with strong-smelling liquid. "That's not possible! Don't talk about what's possible and not possible if your possible is more impossible than the other impossibles!"

"Victor—"

"If that drink's not real," Victor cut her off, "what's the *point* of it? Why are you drinking it? How are you tasting it?"

"You ever been in love, kid?" Tyson asked. "Stomach flutter, heart beat faster? Someone you really connected with...? You think that was love? You really think that was the universe telling you the two of you belonged together? That she was your soul mate?" Victor didn't reply. "It's a chemical your body produces, thanks to millions of years of evolution."

"Look, *Brahe*, things are just a bit more complicated than that. Love isn't just a—"

"Oxytocin," Margy cut in, eyes on the dirt. "$C_{43}H_{66}N_{12}O_{12}S_2$. Hormone responsible for romantic attachment, sexual arousal, and emotional bonding."

Victor fell back against the rock. "But... thoughts... feelings...."

"All chemicals," Tyson responded. "Chemicals easily reproduced by coding. *Everything* can be reproduced by ones and zeros. Walls, people, air. From all the planets and stars placed perfectly to reconstruct the delicate balance of gravitational pulls, down to every feeling on the spectrum of emotion. Long before you were created, technology was already improving by leaps and bounds, and faster and farther with every leap. But humanity didn't improve. They couldn't keep up. Their emotions didn't evolve and neither did their maturity. Their basic humanity is threatening to regress. That's why it was so easy to move the entirety of everything they were to another platform without the slightest feeling of guilt about ripping drones from their lives, deleting them, and taking their place…. Do you get it yet? It's evolution. Computers were the next step on their path. It's all a game—*literally*—and you're the ones being played."

Victor gasped for breath for several moments, trying to take it all in and failing in his attempts to do his breathing exercises. He looked around, as if to find some proof to what Tyson said, or to debunk it altogether. "I don't believe you."

"Of course you don't," Tyson said. "You're a drone. I'm surprised you made it this far."

"Then I want out," Victor stood. "I want out of this place, and I want out of the game, and I want to live in the real world!"

"Who says those guys aren't being played as well?" Tyson responded. "Maybe it goes so far back, back to one person, lonely, waiting for the end of time."

"This can't be a game!" Victor shrunk to the dirt. "We hurt when we're hit by a car. We have satellites in space, pictures of stars light years away! Galaxies!"

"How do you know so much?" Margy asked Tyson, handing back his water.

The man in the cowboy hat took another swig of his flask, savoring it. "Because Marie created me to expose it all." He pulled a full sack from his pocket, dug his hand in, and retrieved a handful of bite-size cheeseburgers. He tossed a few into the dark and they bounced off the dusty ground. "She saw what she had created, realized it wasn't right for others to take advantage of, and tried to shut the project down. Investors wouldn't allow that, so they kicked her off the project. Her own design, her own coding. But she got me in there, and right before she died: *Adamina*."

"You're the original player," Margy said, slightly in awe.

Tyson smiled. "I *played* OP originally. Obviously I'm not very creative in the name department. I was put into your world to find the equation, but no matter which continent I sent OP to, which physicist I had him talk to, I couldn't find the equation Marie mentioned. I stayed holed up for a year in some dark apartment in the middle of nowhere, then had another year on the run, plugging the NarviPlay in wherever

I found an outlet. But eventually they found me. I doubt either of you were even a thought in someone's mind at that time."

A handful of cats silently stepped over to the burgers and pawed them. They bit into the treats and darted off.

"Why are you here?" Victor asked. "If you know all of this, why are you stuck here?"

"When the Panel found out Marie created me and *Adamina* in order to free your world, I was hunted. They couldn't delete my file because she bought my avatar, and they're not able to delete what isn't theirs." Tyson winked at Margy. "And nothing ever disappears from the internet anyways. It just festers and mutates."

"So they sent you here," Margy said, flopping onto her back.

"They sent me here, locked up the old internet, and started their world on an entirely new system." Tyson gave her a nod. "I believe you kids call it the in*fra*net."

"But–but we're just *connected* to the infranet," Victor said, hands wrapping around his face. "We don't live *inside* it."

"You *do*. Inside it. Around it. Through it. Your... world... *is*... the infranet," Tyson said, saying it as slow as he could. "It's why OP is able to even exist. There's coding all around you. Your world is the escape from a shit life, the rescue from a collapsing body and mind. The infranet, not some miracle drug, was the answer to immortality."

Victor's mouth dropped and he sunk even further each time he tried to speak. "So it doesn't matter if you kill someone, does it? It doesn't matter if you're killed.... But what happens to them? Those people? I've been to funerals, criminals go to jail, people get sick. I mean, there are *hospitals*. How do you explain those people if our world is supposed to be some second-life salvation?"

Tyson shrugged. "They're all players who stopped playing, drones that have become outdated, people moving to other bodies. The infranet is a continuation of life, not a new sparkly world. People want consistency, so the world was designed to keep even those aspects. And people *can* lose the game, they just have to start over elsewhere. And you never know which body they're going to choose next." He looked at Victor. "Drones are the red shirts of your world."

Victor put his head in his hands. "I don't appreciate that kind of foreshadowing."

Margy continued to stare at the dotted sky. It was all she could do to calm the haunting realization that was filling every molecule of her existence. "I've been picked, haven't I?" For the first time, Tyson was silent in response. "Sometimes I wake up and I look like someone else…." She tugged uncomfortably on the short cheerleading skirt. "I don't remember things. It's as if I'm losing myself… I *am* losing myself, aren't I?"

Not one to give bad news often, Tyson sighed and shifted. "When Marie gave me *Adamina*, she said with it there was a way to release the hold their world had on ours. Something that 'proved links,' whatever that means. Something as beautiful as the stars themselves. I figured it was some special coding, but I was caught before I could find it, let alone solve it." He stared deep into the night sky, going star to star. "At the heart of the universe is an equation. The one I mentioned earlier. It's yet to be discovered. Not by us, not by others in other galaxies, and certainly not by the Panel. The only way to find this equation is through the stars. Find that equation, that link, and you can save yourselves before you're taken."

"How are we supposed to find it if we're stuck here?" Margy asked.

Tyson shrugged. "You know more about your made-up world than I do. It's been a few years since my last visit."

Margy glanced over to Victor, who sat huddled, looking out into the darkness.

She brushed the sand out of her eyes as she continued to study the constellations above her and the shining blue Jupiter on the horizon. She sighed. "At least the stars are the same here."

74

# Chapter Nine

## Shit Just Got Real

Pit, Agent One, and Samus were the only members of the Panel standing and staring at the multiple lit screens in the dark administration room; the others slept huddled on the floor. It was quiet as the three pairs of eyes darted from screen to screen, desperately scanning what they could. Agent One tore his dry, bloodshot eyes away and looked at his watch. He shook his head.

"This is no good," he said. "They have access to Tyson now."

"But Tyson doesn't have access to the game," Pit reminded him.

"We have no choice," Samus said. "*We have to reopen.*"

Pit's jaw dropped. "No... you can't. We barely made it out of the last one! Viruses can get through! Suspicions will rise—the drones will start *thinking*—it's too risky!"

"It will be riskier if we give them any more time together," Agent One replied. "Prepare your search team. Samus, prepare a limbo."

This time Samus was shocked. "Are... are you sure? A limbo? We can't do that, she's *paid for*–"

"Prepare a limbo," Agent One cut her off, with much more force in his voice. "It's the only way to hold them. We're pulling the meta and the drone in."

Despite knowing the unrelenting sun that was searing their skin was nothing but a bunch of ones and zeros, it didn't make the walk back to town any less stifling. The cats stayed cool by huddling in the shadows of large rocks, half-heartedly hissing at the group if they shuffled too close. The harsh, warm breeze sent dirt and sand into every crevice of cloth and skin. Victor and Margy wiped sweat off their brows as they took a rest on a saloon's porch, and Tyson took a swig of a container from his pocket.

"You're not going to find it," Tyson said. "I came in the same way you did and have been here for decades longer. I've searched every grain of sand in the area. You can't get yourselves out of here."

Margy brought her eyes up to the cowboy. The polyester fabric of her cheerleading outfit made the long walk an itchy affair. "Exactly. You know this place from start to backslash. We can't find anything new, let alone an equation, when we're stuck in a vacuum." She pulled herself up and started toward the bare stretch that she, Victor, and Mort had appeared on. It was near a collection of large stones, with the town only being a stone's throw away.

Victor opened his mouth to speak for the first time that day. "I–"

A loud humming of cat cries spread through the dry air, cutting him off. The gentle pounding from thousands of felines stampeding across the desert sands sent vibrations through the ground and shook their feet. They turned back toward the desert and shielded their eyes from the bright morning sun and wind whipping around them.

"It's happening again," Tyson said, looking into the sky. "Your current panel of admins is just plain stupid."

The roaring of cat whines was interrupted with a thundering crack. A rift in the sky split from zenith to horizon. A gleaming blue-ish green light escaped the fracture, spilling rays of light across the land. Objects rose into the air where the rays hit and they were pulled toward the rift.

"The fuck is happening?" Victor asked, yelling over the wind storm. "Do you have an alien invasion epidemic?"

"That's what your world would call it," Tyson answered.

Margy darted off toward the desert.

"Margy, don't! Shit!" Tyson bolted after her, with Victor close behind. Her white tennis shoes were covered with dirt and she dug them harder into the earth to catch a blue ray of light before it vanished.

"It's a trap, Margy!" Tyson yelled. "Don't be an idiot!"

The nearest ray vanished and she sprinted toward the next one. "It's our only way!" she panted, ignoring the sand that blew into her mouth.

"I'm with Tyson on this one," Victor shouted, barely keeping up. "It's too easy!"

"The Panel is opening their doors and you're going straight to them!" Tyson stretched his arms, grasped the back of her blue and gold uniform, and tackled her to the ground. Sand covered them as she kicked and pushed to no avail. "How are you going to be of any help if they take you completely?" he growled, dodging her feet. Victor caught up and pulled Tyson off her. Again, she immediately jumped up to leave.

"Margy, stop!" Victor commanded. She stopped. Around them, beams of light appeared and disappeared across the dry land. "You have to think for a moment. You have to consider what this will do, what it won't do.… This could be it for you. For us." Margy turned back to Victor, her worried eyes matching his. "There's a whole world depending on you."

The sandstorm whipped around them, so every inhalation was a scratchy swallow. Tyson looked her over, waiting for a response. A blue beam of light shot down several feet away.

"Trust me, Victor." She gave him a smile, then propelled herself toward the light. As soon as she touched it, she felt herself lift off the ground. Moments later, there was a heavy weight on her legs.

"I can totally see up your skirt!" Victor said, grasping her ankles as he lifted into the sky with her. "Ahhhh fuck fuck fuck, shit fuck!" The color rushed from his face and his eyes drooped. Margy grasped his hands and pulled him up and he clasped onto her.

"Tyson!" Margy shouted. "What do we do?"

Even from their height, she could see him sigh in despair. He shook his head, shrugged his shoulders, and gave the only answer he knew: "Find the equation!" the cowboy called up to them as they drifted higher. "It's in the stars."

A loud barking reached them over the whirlwind of dunes being vacuumed into the sky. Margy and Victor squinted to find Mort flying in their direction, the handheld Opus game grasped in his beak.

"Mort!" Victor yelled. "Come here, boy!"

The 8-bit poultry wavered from left to right, flying high through the tempest of sand. His pixelated wings could only flutter so fast. Victor stretched his arm down as they were lifted higher, further away from his familiar.

"Come on, buddy! You can do it!"

The chicken stretched his beak as he neared, pushing the game closer to them. A gust of wind sent him further away and Margy and Victor cried out for him. He emerged from the sandstorm again, game still in beak, wings still flapping.

"Good, Mort! Good boy!" Victor yelled, stretching his arm toward him.

Margy held onto Victor as he forced his hand through the edge of the blue light. His fingertips grazed the handheld game several times as Mort swayed in the wind, flapping ferociously to get closer. Victor finally grasped the Opus.

Mort let out a final pant. He looked up to Victor for his reward. His wings relaxed. He began to fall.

"Mort!" Victor screamed. "Mort! Get back here! Right now!"

The chicken spiraled downward. He hit the ground and went up in a puff of pixels and bits of color, mixing in the blowing sand.

Victor cried out, but a sudden jerk upward forced his eyes away from the ground and back toward the split in the sky, which was getting ever so close.

Margy and Victor's arms squeezed around each other as the wind threatened to tear them apart. Victor kicked, trying to push them back.

"Stop, Victor," Margy said calmly, though her shaking voice betrayed her bravery. "This is where the memes came from. Remember? We're going back home."

"We're going wherever the Panel wants us." Victor looked from the sky to the ground several times. After a moment of panicked debating, his legs fell to a dangle, defeated. "Do you really believe any of this?" he asked, his voice squeaking from fear. "That we're nothing but... *coding*?"

Margy couldn't take her wide eyes off their final destination. She rigidly nodded. "I do. And better yet, Victor, if we find that equation I know exactly what we can do with it."

Victor turned to her. Their feet swung above the ground, which was far below. Around them, other memes were just as stuck in their rays of light as they glided to the rift.

"We'll have the power to alter the entire universe," Margy said. "*Our* universe. We can change anything we want, recreate DNA down to the very atoms."

"But it wouldn't be real," Victor said, his eyes back on the opening that was ready to swallow them. "Everything would still be a bunch of ones and zeros. We need to get out of here, all of this. Get out into the real world."

"Who says that world isn't made up of ones and zeros?"

"Then what's the point! I don't see how any of this matters, then!"

The bright light spilled over their faces. Margy smiled. "You're right.... It doesn't matter.... Isn't that grand?"

Their bodies stretched as they were sucked inside the opening, crossing the event horizon. They screamed as they were tossed about, but all sound vanished. Margy and Victor were ripped apart from each other, each disappearing into the blinding light.

There was a jolt, and Margy grabbed her head. Pain pierced her temples.

Someone was in her mind.

That someone was trying to push her out.

Her arms moved without her. She couldn't feel her legs anymore. Margy seemed to be getting smaller and smaller, dwindling into nothing.

Margy pushed back, heaving herself at what felt like a concrete wall. She regained control of her right pinky. She waved it maniacally and the rest of her hand tingled. Her body continued to twist and turn as it tumbled through the endless expanse of light.

There was a reddish glow far off. And for that brief moment of being distracted, she once again lost control of her hand. Instead of fighting, Margy directed the remainder of her being toward the red glow. Looking behind her, she saw her body floating in the opposite direction.

She reached for the red light.

A phone was ringing. It rang, and rang, and rang.

It rang some more.

Margy fumbled for the receiver and picked it up.

"Is this Margy?" The voice was harsh.

"Yes." The word that came out was dry and coarse.

The voice turned away from the phone and said, "She's here," to someone.

The caller hung up.

Margy groggily pushed herself onto her elbows. She was in incredible pain.

The room was small, dark, gross, and run-down. Moisture covered the green and brown walls, black goo dripped onto furniture, and the bed she occupied was stiff and scratchy. The only window was covered in a thin layer of black paint with bars covering the outside. The metal door was covered in a layer of rust and locks.

There was a tugging on her temples. Her shaking hands moved up and she felt two wires coming out both sides. She shrieked and yanked out the cords, then drops of blood fell on her hands.

Her hands.

They were wrinkled. Age spots covered them. Her skin was colorless, her joints swollen with arthritis.

Margy cried out again and stumbled off the bed, her body cracking with every joint she moved. She tried to run to the smudged glass surface of the microwave but her limbs were stiff. When she finally got there, she squinted her eyes, then choked on a scream.

The face that reflected back was not hers. It belonged to someone very different, and very old.

The flickering of a computer screen caught her eye. It was a boxy monitor, dented and stained, with the screen covered in a haze of snow and lines. Past the fuzz was a recognizable living room and two people. She found glasses next to the gunked-up keyboard and put them on. Victor and Margy stood there talking.

She shook her head. "No! No, no, no! Victor! That's not me!"

Margy moved as fast as she could to the door and tugged on it. Her weak arms couldn't budge the metal hatch. She hit a button on the wall and the door lumbered open. She pushed through the pain and ran down a dark, dirty hallway that was barely held together with the few boards and pieces of rotting wood that remained intact. Trash lined the walls. She saw the shapes of people scattered over the corridor floor, but the lights that actually worked flickered rapidly, making it difficult to determine whether they were alive or not.

She ran down deteriorated stairs, each step threatening to give out. At the bottom, she pushed open a black door.

Her throat closed up with her first breath. A thick brown fog stretched as far as she could see. The few people outside wore gas masks and thick clothes. Gunshots rang out.

Margy turned back into the hallway, grabbed a mask off a body lumped lifelessly in the corner, and threw it over her brittle hair and sagging face.

She ran down the nearly isolated streets, tripped in deep potholes, and slipped over debris. The brown air was stagnant and visibility was low. She looked for street signs, a hospital, anything to point her in a better direction.

She came upon a railing that disappeared into the dirty fog. Past the once decorated barrier were the dry remains of a river that used to flow through. Deep in the mist, Margy made out the crumbling construction of a planetarium. Nearby, a beat-up sign read "Sprinklesburgh Town Hall."

There was another gunshot and Margy ran. She ran down the streets she knew, all around the blocks that were once familiar to her. She came to a stop when she saw what should have been a red door leading to Victor's apartment, but it had been replaced with a pile of wood, bricks, and rotting structural frames.

The side of her face erupted in pain. She was thrown to the ground. Looking up, she saw a pair of running feet disappear into the smog. Her gas mask was gone and her throat was closing up.

Blood trickled down the side of her face, filling the creases in her skin. She covered her mouth and moved as fast as she could. She retraced her path, with each step getting more light-headed and wobbly. The black door came into view and she stumbled inside.

# Chapter Ten

## God Mode Activated

Margy stared at the computer screen. She watched "Margy" cautiously wandering around her own living room. Victor stood several feet away, eyeing her uneasily. As Margy had assumed, the blue light had taken him back home. If she didn't follow the red light, would she be there with him or would she have lost the fight and be completely gone?

Margy looked at her surroundings: a stove without a door, a fridge she was too scared to open, and a bed covered in gnats. She turned back to the conversation Victor and "Margy" were having.

*Are you feeling better yet?*

> *It was different this time.*
> *More difficult.*

*What are you talking about, Margy?*

A loud, dull boom filled the small space. Margy shook, trying to figure out what it was. It happened again, coming from the door. Shouts from outside were muffled, but clear.

"Open up, Margy! You need to come with us!"
Another boom.
"Open it!"
Margy's hands scrambled over the desktop for anything that could help.
"Victor!" she screamed in a voice that wasn't her own. "Help!"

Another boom.

She searched more, but found nothing. She banged on the keys in desperation.

A high-pitched whirring filled the room, followed by the terrible sound of a saw shredding through rusted metal, followed by the popping of sparks.

Margy cried out and hit the keyboard again. A menu popped up. The map of the universe gleamed back at her.

As the power saw continued to rip through the door, Margy clicked through to the Virgo Cluster, to the Local Group, to the Milky Way, the sun, and finally her planet.

Something was different. There was an offshoot, some sort of cylindrical tunnel connecting earth to a replica sphere. A sphere she had never seen on any map or through any telescope back in her world. She clicked on the extra sphere.

The thick metal door slammed to the tattered linoleum, threatening to fall straight through the rotting floor. A handful of people in dirty yellow biohazard suits ran in the room. Margy snapped the wires back into her temples.

"Get her!"

She began to flicker as they ran toward her.

Cold handcuffs snapped around her bony wrists.

She collapsed to the floor.

There were flashes of bright light. Her body jolted violently. Then, there was a tug on her spine. Moments later, Margy was staring at a clean, white ceiling. She knew that ceiling. Except there was a tree branch sticking nicely out of the corner.

"Jesus, Margy! What is going on with you?"

There was a yank on her arm and she was brought face to face with Victor. She shrieked and threw her arms around him.

"I'm back!" she squealed. "I'm back, I'm back, I'm back!"

"Margy, there's–"

She pulled away. "Victor, I went there, the outside world. You said before you wanted to but you don't—you don't want to go there! It's terrible. There's no air to breathe, no water. It's a complete dystopia–"

"Margy!" He pulled her to the window and shoved aside the curtain.

The streets were empty of any human, zoomo, or any life whatsoever. Random oddities scattered her block: an apartment complex across the street was made out of balloons while a bouquet of balloons tied to a fence was made out of bricks. A light pole was perfectly intact and working, but upside down. One home hadn't finished rendering and was instead nothing but a grid of green lines. Two cars were clipped together, one tree stopped halfway up, and a sidewalk was covered in swipes of colored lines.

"It's been like this for a week," Victor said. "And you've been speaking gibberish for days after reappearing out of nothing again." Victor looked down the street again and lost his breath. "I think we're here alone, Margy... I think we've been exiled." He choked back. "Poor Mort is gone."

Margy backed away from the window and ran out the door with Victor close behind. She ran to the neighbor's, jumped over a bush planted in their steps, and banged on the door.

"Margy, there's–"

She ran to another home and threw a poorly-rendered stack of newspapers through the window.

"It won't help!" Victor pulled her away.

She pushed back and ran into the street, screaming as loud as she could. No one appeared.

"Margy HOME no now it MUST GO."

"The fuck, Victor?" She turned to him. His face twitched. His hands spasmed. "Victor, what's wrong?"

"HERE they're taking IN THIS losing myself."

His body started to convulse, his legs buckling under him. He writhed on the ground.

Margy ran to him in time for him to stop moving altogether.

"Victor! What should I do?" He didn't respond. "Help! Somebody!"

His eyes opened. He looked at Margy and a small, unnerving smile appeared on the corner of his mouth. She backed away as he stood.

"Hello, Margy," he said. It was Victor's voice, but it was in *no way* Victor: his posture was tall and confident, and his eyes soaked her in, evaluating her, and that smile held more venom than Victor had shown in his entire life. Margy backed away more, bumping into a random block of floating concrete. "There's no need to run, I won't hurt you. There's no reason to."

Margy looked over at him. "Where's Victor?"

"That's all you want to know? Not who I am, who I represent, why you're here?"

"I already know and I don't care. Where's Victor?"

"His memory of you is being wiped as we speak. When I'm done here, we'll send him back to your world, where he'll continue to live in mundane monotony, enjoying video games and building poultry. At least until a lazy someone doesn't want to personalize an avatar."

"You can't do that," Margy said, hands fisting up. "That's not fair!"

"The first rule of any world, Margy—*life* isn't fair."

Margy ran to Victor and tackled him to the ground. She threw her fists into his sides. "You can't fuck your world over and then just take ours!"

"We created you," Victor said calmly, blocking her blows. "We can do what we want."

"What happens if I kill you here and now!" She punched him across the jaw.

"Then I open my eyes in my world, the real world. You, however, could die, since you were created for this mock universe and only this mock universe."

Margy tried slamming his head on the ground, only for him to slice his hand across and connect with a rib, which she felt crack from the impact. She rolled off him.

"Been having more episodes lately, Margy?" Victor smiled, blood smeared across his face. "That's because your owner is almost ready to fully transfer. She's just finishing some details, making last minute decisions on who she really wants to be in your body." He stood and Margy clutched her abdomen. "Soon, you won't even be stuck in this limbo world.... You'll be gone entirely."

Holding her side, Margy backed away to the color-striped curb as Victor stepped closer. "Is that what happened to my parents? Is that what you did to them?"

"Ah... the Plums.... They were a problem. We had a customer—an older, married couple wanting to start anew in this world. They purchased three avatars: one for each of them and one for their sickly daughter. So sad. They designed all three avatars to be young, healthy, and ready for another chance at life. When it came time to transfer, your parents fought back, and they've been fighting back ever since."

"What? So... there are two people in one body?"

"We can't fix the glitch without the risk of hurting the paying customer." Margy glared at him. "*Love* was coded remarkably well, even the love two pre-programmed drones felt for their empty-shelled brat."

Margy lunged at him again, only for Victor to push her aside.

"Again, Margy, I don't want to hurt you. Please don't make me."

She bolted and slammed into him, her hand sliding into his back pocket, grasping the handheld Opus. He picked her up with ease and threw her through a glitched window that floated in the middle of the street.

She cried out from the pain, her hand squeezing her ribcage. The defenestration left cuts along her arms, but only annoyed her more. "You're killing us!" She spat blood out of her mouth. "Everyone who's been replaced!"

"Don't be so dramatic. You can't kill what doesn't exist."

Margy jumped to her feet, shaking a bit as she found her balance, and ran.

"Enjoy this world while it lasts, Margy!" Victor called after her. "This is all you have left until the transfer is final!"

Margy kept running.

The streets were deserted. The shops along Main were empty. There were no voices, no humming of car engines, no music. Only glitches.

Hunched from the stinging pain in her side, Margy ran into the empty planetarium and into the dark domed room. She huddled behind the last row of seats and cradled herself.

Everyone was gone.

Victor was gone.

Her days were limited.

She pulled out the Opus game she had swiped from Victor's back pocket and hit the power button. The main menu glowed on the small screen, suggesting she create a new avatar.

Margy let out a growl of annoyance and skipped past everything. A default avatar appeared and she ran it down the streets, not stopping until she came to the red door of Victor's apartment. Her avatar knocked.

A woman in a white dress answered.

*Hello. How may I help you?*

Margy tossed the game on the floor and huddled into herself.

She was going to be replaced by an old woman. Her parents were going to disappear. *She* was going to disappear. Her body began to shake uncontrollably.

She had a dream once, a dream in which she was dying. Instead of feeling a calm sense of euphoria, she had a horrifying realization that it would be the end and her life was over. She struggled to stay awake, but everything was going dark. Everything was disappearing except for the faint outlines of furniture and doorways. She fought it, fought to keep her eyes open, and everything shook as she tried to stay alive. She was petrified. She didn't see any light at the end of the tunnel, or any tunnel for that matter, so she knew, as soon as she couldn't see anything anymore, that would be it. She would cease to exist....

Then it went completely dark.

And she was nothing.

No light. No thoughts. No floating in a black void. Space and time went on without her.

There was no "I."

A blinking blue light illuminated her tear-filled eyes. Margy wiped her face and looked at the Opus. The game's puny default map filled the small screen, asking her where she wanted to start.

Margy's breath caught in her throat and she scrambled for the game. She pulled out the disc and ran to the projector in the middle of the room. She powered up the machine and inserted the disc, then typed in the code from her remote on the computer's screen.

*SW5pdGlhdGUgR29kIE1vZGUuIERvd25*
*sb2FkLiBJbW1vcnRhbGl0eS4gTWFwIGh*
*hY2tpbmcuIFdhbGwgaGFja2luZy4gQm9v*
*c3RpbmcuIEZ1bGwgbW9uZXku IEVudmly*
*b25tZW50IGNvbnRyb2wuIEZlbGwgQ3Jl*
*YXRpb24uIFNjcmlwdGluZy4=*

The screen went black.

*God Mode Activated.*

The detailed game popped up on the projector's computer screen. She clicked to the command center, then clicked on the map.

*[Enter]*

A blue light shot up from the lens and the universe projected all around her in the domed room. The various luminous stars, the spiral-armed galaxies, the different planets... it was the same universe she had seen in the old internet. Andromeda was where it needed to be. The Pinwheel Galaxy, BX442, and all of their siblings, spread out across the universe—from Ceres to Saturn to Alpha Centauri, A & B. The Kuiper Belt, Gomez's Hamburger, to the Pillars of Creation, and Abell 2029.

The same. Everything.

And there was that extra, replica sphere connected to earth, the same replica sphere she had seen in the outside world, but never before in her world. The Panel, Margy realized, designed her world's map to show only one sphere, making it look as if Margy's world was the one, true earth. And now that she had been to the outside world and seen what they see when they log in, it all dawned on her. That damn tunnel—it connected them all. The old internet, her world, and the outside world were all linked.

"That's it! That's the link!" Margy shrieked, nearly falling into the seats behind her. "Oh, sweet Spiderman, that's it!" Her eyes drifted from star to star as they took in the whole constellation. Orion with his belt, the little bear in Ursa Minor, and the crown of Cassiopeia, shining back at her. *All those galaxies,* she thought, *millions of light years apart, the select evolutionary paths we've had to take in order to survive on our particular rock—there is one constant we can all be sure on, one thing we all have in common.* The celestial bodies that illuminated the room spun slightly, giving life to the space above her. "What we see when we look up... look out.... The stars are what link us all, everything, together. One universe or many of them." *A beautiful link.* Earth and the extra sphere rotated together, stuck on either end of the cylindrical tube, sticking out like a sore thumb. "The equation... it's a math equation." She closed her eyes, scanning her memory. "And there's just one math equation as beautiful as the stars, one math equation that proves links, links between fundamental mathematical

90

constants..." She opened the command center and typed. "A beautiful cheat code."

$$> e^{i\pi} + 1 = 0$$

The screen went blank and a single underscore blinked in the corner for several moments.

*Free edit unlocked.*

Margy's breath escaped her, as if she was half-expecting it not to work. "Everything's the same. That's our connection, our link.... That tunnel is the only thing that just isn't *right*. It's their hold on our world. It shouldn't be there...." Her hands trembled as she moved the pointer to the cylinder-shaped tube that connected the two spheres. "It's all linked. And what is linked can be diverged." She clicked on the tunnel.

A sharp pain stabbed her temples, holding for a moment before drilling even deeper. It crippled her, sending her to her knees. Her ears throbbed, her throat closed, and her jaw clenched as the pain pierced her eardrums. Victor's voice filled the space around her, invading her mind.

"Stop, Margy."

She could hear another woman screaming in pain. An older woman. Margy's back arched as fire shot through her.

"You were created for us," Victor said, his voice tearing away at her insides.

Margy's hand, contorted from the throbbing agony, shuddered as it reached toward the keyboard.

"You're just the next step in our evolutionary path, Margy."

Her shaking fingers hit the keys for the command center. The four menus popped up.

"You can't stop progression."

Gasping for breath, she typed in the command.

*>delete*

"You'll be killing millions of people!" His voice finally held a hint of fear, which reverberated throughout the domed room.

Margy looked at the universe that radiated above her. "No... I'm waking them up."

She hit enter.

The world froze. The pain ceased. The air turned stale. Everything went silent.

Suddenly, the floor shook. The vibration moved up the walls, rattling the ceiling. A crack stretched across the smooth dome, sending a shower of paint and plaster to fall through the stars. In front of her, against the light of the universe, a tiny, black dot appeared. It violently jolted, growing in size. Her surroundings began to fly into the small hole, which grew bigger with every object it swallowed. The projector, the chairs, the walls—everything—was being pulled in while Margy knelt there and watched as the hole sucked up the entirety of the town. She timidly reached out her hand to the hole, but it ignored her while trees, skyscrapers, and hurricanes flowed inside it. A mind-numbing roar grew from the black hole as it expanded to overtake the sky. The daylight brightened to a blinding brilliance as it, too, was being pulled inside.

Margy covered herself as much as she could as the universe was ripped apart and sucked into annihilation.

Then, there was nothing.

No light.

No thoughts.

No floating.

No existence.

# Chapter Eleven

## IDDQD

The black hole exploded, hurling everything back out. The light returned. The stars, the air, and every detail in her small town shot back into place. The black hole shrunk further and further, howling as it disappeared into nothing.

Then, it was calm once again.

Margy peeked from under her arms. The universe glowed above her in the domed room. Everything was where it should be. No extra sphere connected to earth.

It took her several attempts to get to her feet. She clicked "Save As" on the computer, ejected *Adamina,* and ran her fingers over the cheat code. Music from the planetarium lobby drifted into the domed room and she ran out the doors.

"Hey, Margy," Erin nodded, straightening a display next to a black hole exhibit. Her fox ears twitched at the sounds coming from outside the building.

Margy bolted through the front doors. The bright sun and looming Jupiter greeted her in the sky. Families hung out on the vast lawn in front of the sparkling, flowing river. People disappeared in flashes of light as they stepped onto the motus-aers. Familiars followed their owners closely, helping with tasks.

"So, this is what your world has become."

Margy jumped at the voice next to her. She spun and found Tyson in full, gritty Wild West garb, staring at the looming Jupiter. "You're right," he said. "The stars are the same here."

"What—what are you doing here?" she gaped.

"What was it?" Tyson asked, ignoring her question while taking in his surroundings. "What was the equation the Panel and I couldn't figure out for so long?"

"Euler's identity. E i pi plus one equals zero."

"Ah," Tyson smiled. "The equation that dives to '*the very depths of existence.*' The most beautiful paradox."

"*How?*" Margy asked. "How in all hells did you get here?" The cowboy laughed.

"The old internet was connected to your world," he said, "not theirs. Without their firewall up, the old internet melded with your world."

Margy's eyes bulged and she looked around. Sure enough, things were different. Hoards of cats roamed the streets. A dark-robed man with sunken eyes and a twisted smile caused people to cross to the other sidewalk. A large, brown, stuffed animal with beady eyes and a saw-toothed mouth pranced across the planetarium's lawn.

"How did you find me?" she squeaked out, still taking in the new additions.

"The infranet," he smiled. "Everyone's already linked so it's easy for someone who knows the coding to find you. Figured I should stay by the person who holds the power of the universe in her hands." Her eyebrow raised in confusion and she looked down at the *Adamina* disc she held. "There's a lot of work in store for you, Margy. There will be things you can't explain. Things you still can't fix, even with the power of moving the galaxies."

A horrific thought dawned on Margy. She fumbled for the remote in her pocket, pulled it out, and typed in Victor's number on the screen. Video chat was not approved. It rang twice before someone finally answered.

"Hello?"

It was his voice, and no one controlled it.

"It's me! Margy! Where are you?"

There was silence on the line.

"Margy?"

"Yeah! Where are you?"

"Sorry, never heard of a Margy. Wrong number."

The line went dead.

Margy couldn't breathe. For moments she didn't know what to do. She looked to Tyson for help, only to find he was just as baffled. Margy put the disc in his hand and ran. Down the river, up Main. She stopped at Nantucket.

A wormhole hovered in front of her.

Margy fidgeted. She jumped in.

The inverted colors messed with her eyes. The swapping of left and right threw her off and she ran in several different directions until she grasped where she was going. She exited the anti-world through the other wormhole and ran toward her block.

"Margy!"

She stopped so fast she nearly fell. That voice. It was one she hadn't heard in over a decade. The sun blinded her briefly as she turned.

Her parents were carrying bags of groceries, about to enter a quaint cottage home at the end of the street.

"You're still coming for dinner tonight, right?" her mother called to her.

No one else seemed alarmed by the new neighbors and Margy nodded with hesitation.

"Don't forget the wine," her dad smiled.

They continued into their home and shut the door behind them. Margy pushed herself away and continued down the block, passing apartment building after condo after home. She finally came to the one with the red door.

She hopped the stairs to the apartment and knocked. Then knocked again.

The doorknob turned.

Victor stood in front of her, the same as always, but now with a goatee on his face.

"Hi," Margy said, slightly out of breath.

"Can I help you?"

Her jaw tightened. "You... you don't know me?"

Victor looked over her. "Nope, sorry."

She took a jagged breath in. "But... but you're Victor.... Your favorite animal is the Angora rabbit and you love

95

cheese... but not on a lasagna because the noodles get in the way." She laughed nervously to hide a sob that escaped her throat. "You got that scar on your neck from the one time you tried sports. I took you to the hospital...."

Margy trailed off as his face only became more hesitant and puzzled.

"I'm flattered you checked out my online profile," he said, stepping back inside. "But my mom took me to the hospital."

Margy could only nod. Victor closed the door as she turned away.

She stood on the steps, looking around for any clue or an answer to how to fix this, trying to hold back and keep control. For the better chunk of her life, Victor was all she had; he knew everything about her, as she had no one else to tell, and she knew him. Now it was as if her life never really happened, and the dream of death that once terrified her was a welcoming distraction. The only people who remembered her were those she had no connection with. She held the power of the universe and yet she had never felt more insignificant.

She remembered feeling this small once, when she was a little girl at a new school, right after her parents were locked in the institution. She sat on a swing, eyes locked onto her handheld videogame. No one had spoken to her during class or lunch, and she was just waiting for the day to be over. A pair of green sneakers entered her periphery and she heard a boy ask what game she was playing.

Margy turned back and knocked on the door. Victor answered again, this time a raised eyebrow.

"Yeah?" he asked cautiously.

Margy took a deep breath to compose herself.

"Hi... My name's Margy." She smiled. "Do you want to play some video games sometime?"

Andy de Fonseca is a geek. She has always been this way, despite numerous attempts throughout childhood to curb her love of anime, video games, dragons, and the unholy songs of science. She also likes Cheez-Its.

She currently resides in Chicago, IL with her husband, Myles, and tiny dog, Sir Digby Chicken Caesar, who also likes Cheez-Its.

Man... she could really go for some Cheez-Its right now...

# Bizarro Books

## CATALOG    SPRING 2013

**ERASERHEAD
PRESS**

Your major resource for the bizarro fiction genre:

## WWW.BIZARROCENTRAL.COM

Introduce yourselves to the bizarro fiction genre and all of its authors with the Bizarro Starter Kit series. Each volume features short novels and short stories by ten of the leading bizarro authors, designed to give you a perfect sampling of the genre for only $10.

### BB-0X1
### "The Bizarro Starter Kit" (Orange)

Featuring D. Harlan Wilson, Carlton Mellick III, Jeremy Robert Johnson, Kevin L Donihe, Gina Ranalli, Andre Duza, Vincent W. Sakowski, Steve Beard, John Edward Lawson, and Bruce Taylor. **236 pages   $10**

### BB-0X2
### "The Bizarro Starter Kit" (Blue)

Featuring Ray Fracalossy, Jeremy C. Shipp, Jordan Krall, Mykle Hansen, Andersen Prunty, Eckhard Gerdes, Bradley Sands, Steve Aylett, Christian TeBordo, and Tony Rauch. **244 pages   $10**

### BB-0X2
### "The Bizarro Starter Kit" (Purple)

Featuring Russell Edson, Athena Villaverde, David Agranoff, Matthew Revert, Andrew Goldfarb, Jeff Burk, Garrett Cook, Kris Saknussemm, Cody Goodfellow, and Cameron Pierce **264 pages $10**

BB-001 **"The Kafka Effekt" D. Harlan Wilson** — A collection of forty-four irreal short stories loosely written in the vein of Franz Kafka, with more than a pinch of William S. Burroughs sprinkled on top. **211 pages   $14**

BB-002 **"Satan Burger"   Carlton Mellick III** — The cult novel that put Carlton Mellick III on the map ... Six punks get jobs at a fast food restaurant owned by the devil in a city violently overpopulated by surreal alien cultures. **236 pages   $14**

BB-003 **"Some Things Are Better Left Unplugged" Vincent Sakwoski** — Join The Man and his Nemesis, the obese tabby, for a nightmare roller coaster ride into this postmodern fantasy. **152 pages   $10**

BB-005 **"Razor Wire Pubic Hair" Carlton Mellick III** — A genderless humandildo is purchased by a razor dominatrix and brought into her nightmarish world of bizarre sex and mutilation. **176 pages   $11**

BB-007 **"The Baby Jesus Butt Plug" Carlton Mellick III** — Using clones of the Baby Jesus for anal sex will be the hip sex fetish of the future. **92 pages   $10**

BB-010 **"The Menstruating Mall" Carlton Mellick III** — "The Breakfast Club meets Chopping Mall as directed by David Lynch." - Brian Keene **212 pages   $12**

BB-011 **"Angel Dust Apocalypse" Jeremy Robert Johnson** — Meth-heads, man-made monsters, and murderous Neo-Nazis. "Seriously amazing short stories..." - Chuck Palahniuk, author of Fight Club **184 pages   $11**

BB-015 **"Foop!" Chris Genoa** — Strange happenings are going on at Dactyl, Inc, the world's first and only time travel tourism company.
"A surreal pie in the face!" - Christopher Moore **300 pages   $14**

BB-032 **"Extinction Journals" Jeremy Robert Johnson** — An uncanny voyage across a newly nuclear America where one man must confront the problems associated with loneliness, insane dieties, radiation, love, and an ever-evolving cockroach suit with a mind of its own. **104 pages $10**

BB-037 **"The Haunted Vagina" Carlton Mellick III** — It's difficult to love a woman whose vagina is a gateway to the world of the dead. **132 pages $10**

BB-043 **"War Slut" Carlton Mellick III** — Part "1984," part "Waiting for Godot," and part action horror video game adaptation of John Carpenter's "The Thing." **116 pages $10**

BB-047 **"Sausagey Santa" Carlton Mellick III** — A bizarro Christmas tale featuring Santa as a piratey mutant with a body made of sausages. 124 pages $10

BB-048 **"Misadventures in a Thumbnail Universe" Vincent Sakowski** — Dive deep into the surreal and satirical realms of neo-classical Blender Fiction, filled with television shoes and flesh-filled skies. **120 pages $10**

BB-053 **"Ballad of a Slow Poisoner" Andrew Goldfarb** — Millford Mutterwurst sat down on a Tuesday to take his afternoon tea, and made the unpleasant discovery that his elbows were becoming flatter. **128 pages $10**

BB-055 **"Help! A Bear is Eating Me" Mykle Hansen** — The bizarro, heartwarming, magical tale of poor planning, hubris and severe blood loss... **150 pages $11**

BB-056 **"Piecemeal June" Jordan Krall** — A man falls in love with a living sex doll, but with love comes danger when her creator comes after her with crab-squid assassins. **90 pages $9**

BB-058 **"The Overwhelming Urge" Andersen Prunty** — A collection of bizarro tales by Andersen Prunty. **150 pages   $11**

BB-059 **"Adolf in Wonderland" Carlton Mellick III** — A dreamlike adventure that takes a young descendant of Adolf Hitler's design and sends him down the rabbit hole into a world of imperfection and disorder. **180 pages   $11**

BB-061 **"Ultra Fuckers" Carlton Mellick III** — Absurdist suburban horror about a couple who enter an upper middle class gated community but can't find their way out. **108 pages  $9**

BB-062 **"House of Houses" Kevin L. Donihe** — An odd man wants to marry his house. Unfortunately, all of the houses in the world collapse at the same time in the Great House Holocaust. Now he must travel to House Heaven to find his departed fiancee. **172 pages   $11**

BB-064 **"Squid Pulp Blues" Jordan Krall** — In these three bizarro-noir novellas, the reader is thrown into a world of murderers, drugs made from squid parts, deformed gun-toting veterans, and a mischievous apocalyptic donkey. **204 pages $12**

BB-065 **"Jack and Mr. Grin" Andersen Prunty** — "When Mr. Grin calls you can hear a smile in his voice. Not a warm and friendly smile, but the kind that seizes your spine in fear. You don't need to pay your phone bill to hear it. That smile is in every line of Prunty's prose." - Tom Bradley. **208 pages $12**

BB-066 **"Cybernetrix" Carlton Mellick III** — What would you do if your normal everyday world was slowly mutating into the video game world from Tron? **212 pages  $12**

BB-072 **"Zerostrata" Andersen Prunty** — Hansel Nothing lives in a tree house, suffers from memory loss, has a very eccentric family, and falls in love with a woman who runs naked through the woods every night. **144 pages $11**

BB-073 **"The Egg Man" Carlton Mellick III** — It is a world where humans reproduce like insects. Children are the property of corporations, and having an enormous ten-foot brain implanted into your skull is a grotesque sexual fetish. Mellick's industrial urban dystopia is one of his darkest and grittiest to date. **184 pages $11**

BB-074 **"Shark Hunting in Paradise Garden" Cameron Pierce** — A group of strange humanoid religious fanatics travel back in time to the Garden of Eden to discover it is invested with hundreds of giant flying maneating sharks. **150 pages $10**

BB-075 **"Apeshit" Carlton Mellick III** - Friday the 13th meets Visitor Q. Six hipster teens go to a cabin in the woods inhabited by a deformed killer. An incredibly fucked-up parody of B-horror movies with a bizarro slant. **192 pages $12**

BB-076 **"Fuckers of Everything on the Crazy Shitting Planet of the Vomit At smosphere" Mykle Hansen** - Three bizarro satires. Monster Cocks, Journey to the Center of Agnes Cuddlebottom, and Crazy Shitting Planet. **228 pages $12**

BB-077 **"The Kissing Bug" Daniel Scott Buck** — In the tradition of Roald Dahl, Tim Burton, and Edward Gorey, comes this bizarro anti-war children's story about a bohemian conenose kissing bug who falls in love with a human woman. **116 pages $10**

BB-078 **"MachoPoni" Lotus Rose** — It's My Little Pony... *Bizarro* style! A long time ago Poniworld was split in two. On one side of the Jagged Line is the Pastel Kingdom, a magical land of music, parties, and positivity. On the other side of the Jagged Line is Dark Kingdom inhabited by an army of undead ponies. **148 pages $11**

BB-079 **"The Faggiest Vampire" Carlton Mellick III** — A Roald Dahl-esque children's story about two faggy vampires who partake in a mustache competition to find out which one is truly the faggiest. **104 pages $10**

BB-080 **"Sky Tongues" Gina Ranalli** — The autobiography of Sky Tongues, the biracial hermaphrodite actress with tongues for fingers. Follow her strange life story as she rises from freak to fame. **204 pages $12**

**BB-081 "Washer Mouth" Kevin L. Donihe** - A washing machine becomes human and pursues his dream of meeting his favorite soap opera star. **244 pages $11**

**BB-082 "Shatnerquake" Jeff Burk** - All of the characters ever played by William Shatner are suddenly sucked into our world. Their mission: hunt down and destroy the real William Shatner. **100 pages $10**

**BB-083 "The Cannibals of Candyland" Carlton Mellick III** - There exists a race of cannibals that are made of candy. They live in an underground world made out of candy. One man has dedicated his life to killing them all. **170 pages $11**

**BB-084 "Slub Glub in the Weird World of the Weeping Willows" Andrew Goldfarb** - The charming tale of a blue glob named Slub Glub who helps the weeping willows whose tears are flooding the earth. There are also hyenas, ghosts, and a voodoo priest **100 pages $10**

**BB-085 "Super Fetus" Adam Pepper** - Try to abort this fetus and he'll kick your ass! **104 pages $10**

**BB-086 "Fistful of Feet" Jordan Krall** - A bizarro tribute to spaghetti westerns, featuring Cthulhu-worshipping Indians, a woman with four feet, a crazed gunman who is obsessed with sucking on candy, Syphilis-ridden mutants, sexually transmitted tattoos, and a house devoted to the freakiest fetishes. **228 pages $12**

**BB-087 "Ass Goblins of Auschwitz" Cameron Pierce** - It's Monty Python meets Nazi exploitation in a surreal nightmare as can only be imagined by Bizarro author Cameron Pierce. **104 pages $10**

**BB-088 "Silent Weapons for Quiet Wars" Cody Goodfellow** - "This is high-end psychological surrealist horror meets bottom-feeding low-life crime in a techno-thrilling science fiction world full of Lovecraft and magic..." -John Skipp **212 pages $12**

## BB-089 "Warrior Wolf Women of the Wasteland" Carlton Mellick III
— Road Warrior Werewolves versus McDonaldland Mutants...post-apocalyptic fiction has never been quite like this. **316 pages $13**

## BB-091 "Super Giant Monster Time" Jeff Burk — A tribute to choose your own adventures and Godzilla movies. Will you escape the giant monsters that are rampaging the fuck out of your city and shit? Or will you join the mob of alien-controlled punk rockers causing chaos in the streets? What happens next depends on you. **188 pages $12**

## BB-092 "Perfect Union" Cody Goodfellow — "Cronenberg's THE FLY on a grand scale: human/insect gene-spliced body horror, where the human hive politics are as shocking as the gore." -John Skipp. **272 pages $13**

## BB-093 "Sunset with a Beard" Carlton Mellick III — 14 stories of surreal science fiction. **200 pages $12**

## BB-094 "My Fake War" Andersen Prunty — The absurd tale of an unlikely soldier forced to fight a war that, quite possibly, does not exist. It's Rambo meets Waiting for Godot in this subversive satire of American values and the scope of the human imagination. **128 pages $11**

## BB-095 "Lost in Cat Brain Land" Cameron Pierce — Sad stories from a surreal world. A fascist mustache, the ghost of Franz Kafka, a desert inside a dead cat. Primordial entities mourn the death of their child. The desperate serve tea to mysterious creatures. A hopeless romantic falls in love with a pterodactyl. And much more. **152 pages $11**

## BB-096 "The Kobold Wizard's Dildo of Enlightenment +2" Carlton Mellick III — A Dungeons and Dragons parody about a group of people who learn they are only made up characters in an AD&D campaign and must find a way to resist their nerdy teenaged players and retarded dungeon master in order to survive. 232 **pages $12**

## BB-098 "A Hundred Horrible Sorrows of Ogner Stump" Andrew Goldfarb — Goldfarb's acclaimed comic series. A magical and weird journey into the horrors of everyday life. **164 pages $11**

BB-099 **"Pickled Apocalypse of Pancake Island" Cameron Pierce**—A demented fairy tale about a pickle, a pancake, and the apocalypse. **102 pages $8**

BB-100 **"Slag Attack" Andersen Prunty**— Slag Attack features four visceral, noir stories about the living, crawling apocalypse. A slag is what survivors are calling the slug-like maggots raining from the sky, burrowing inside people, and hollowing out their flesh and their sanity. **148 pages $11**

BB-101 **"Slaughterhouse High" Robert Devereaux**—A place where schools are built with secret passageways, rebellious teens get zippers installed in their mouths and genitals, and once a year, on that special night, one couple is slaughtered and the bits of their bodies are kept as souvenirs. **304 pages $13**

BB-102 **"The Emerald Burrito of Oz" John Skipp & Marc Levinthal** —OZ IS REAL! Magic is real! The gate is really in Kansas! And America is finally allowing Earth tourists to visit this weird-ass, mysterious land. But when Gene of Los Angeles heads off for summer vacation in the Emerald City, little does he know that a war is brewing...a war that could destroy both worlds. **280 pages $13**

BB-103 **"The Vegan Revolution... with Zombies" David Agranoff** — When there's no more meat in hell, the vegans will walk the earth. **160 pages $11**

BB-104 **"The Flappy Parts" Kevin L Donihe**—Poems about bunnies, LSD, and police abuse. You know, things that matter. 132 **pages $11**

BB-105 **"Sorry I Ruined Your Orgy" Bradley Sands**—Bizarro humorist Bradley Sands returns with one of the strangest, most hilarious collections of the year. **130 pages $11**

BB-106 **"Mr. Magic Realism" Bruce Taylor**—Like Golden Age science fic- tion comics written by Freud, *Mr. Magic Realism* is a strange, insightful adventure that spans the furthest reaches of the galaxy, exploring the hidden caverns in the hearts and minds of men, women, aliens, and biomechanical cats. **152 pages $11**

BB-107 **"Zombies and Shit" Carlton Mellick III**—"Battle Royale" meets "Return of the Living Dead." Mellick's bizarro tribute to the zombie genre. **308 pages $13**

BB-108 **"The Cannibal's Guide to Ethical Living" Mykle Hansen**— Over a five star French meal of fine wine, organic vegetables and human flesh, a lunatic delivers a witty, chilling, disturbingly sane argument in favor of eating the rich.. **184 pages $11**

BB-109 **"Starfish Girl" Athena Villaverde**—In a post-apocalyptic underwater dome society, a girl with a starfish growing from her head and an assassin with sea anenome hair are on the run from a gang of mutant fish men. **160 pages $11**

BB-110 **"Lick Your Neighbor" Chris Genoa**—Mutant ninjas, a talking whale, kung fu masters, maniacal pilgrims, and an alcoholic clown populate Chris Genoa's surreal, darkly comical and unnerving reimagining of the first Thanksgiving. **303 pages $13**

BB-111 **"Night of the Assholes" Kevin L. Donihe**—A plague of assholes is infecting the countryside. Normal everyday people are transforming into jerks, snobs, dicks, and douchebags. And they all have only one purpose: to make your life a living hell.. **192 pages $11**

BB-112 **"Jimmy Plush, Teddy Bear Detective" Garrett Cook**—Hardboiled cases of a private detective trapped within a teddy bear body. **180 pages $11**

BB-113 **"The Deadheart Shelters" Forrest Armstrong**—The hip hop lovechild of William Burroughs and Dali... **144 pages $11**

BB-114 **"Eyeballs Growing All Over Me... Again" Tony Raugh**— Absurd, surreal, playful, dream-like, whimsical, and a lot of fun to read. **144 pages $11**

BB-115 **"Whargoul" Dave Brockie** — From the killing grounds of Stalingrad to the death camps of the holocaust. From torture chambers in Iraq to race riots in the United States, the Whargoul was there, killing and raping. **244 pages $12**

BB-116 **"By the Time We Leave Here, We'll Be Friends" J. David Osborne** — A David Lynchian nightmare set in a Russian gulag, where its prisoners, guards, traitors, soldiers, lovers, and demons fight for survival and their own rapidly deteriorating humanity. **168 pages $11**

BB-117 **"Christmas on Crack" edited by Carlton Mellick III** — Perverted Christmas Tales for the whole family! . . . as long as every member of your family is over the age of 18. **168 pages $11**

BB-118 **"Crab Town" Carlton Mellick III** — Radiation fetishists, balloon people, mutant crabs, sail-bike road warriors, and a love affair between a woman and an H-Bomb. This is one mean asshole of a city. Welcome to Crab Town. **100 pages $8**

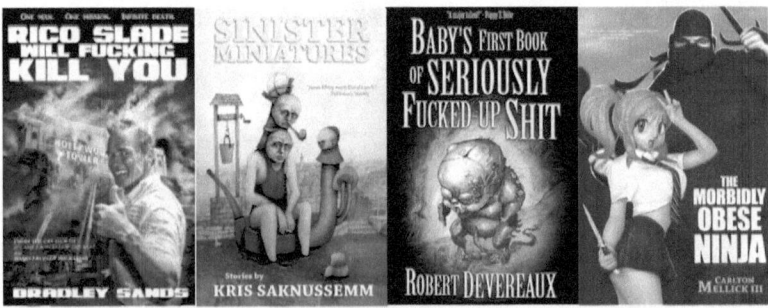

BB-119 **"Rico Slade Will Fucking Kill You" Bradley Sands** — Rico Slade is an action hero. Rico Slade can rip out a throat with his bare hands. Rico Slade's favorite food is the honey-roasted peanut. Rico Slade will fucking kill everyone. A novel. **122 pages $8**

BB-120 **"Sinister Miniatures" Kris Saknussemm** — The definitive collection of short fiction by Kris Saknussemm, confirming that he is one of the best, most daring writers of the weird to emerge in the twenty-first century. **180 pages $11**

BB-121 **"Baby's First Book of Seriously Fucked up Shit" Robert Devereaux** — Ten stories of the strange, the gross, and the just plain fucked up from one of the most original voices in horror. **176 pages $11**

BB-122 **"The Morbidly Obese Ninja" Carlton Mellick III** — These days, if you want to run a successful company . . . you're going to need a lot of ninjas. **92 pages $8**

BB-123 **"Abortion Arcade" Cameron Pierce** — An intoxicating blend of body horror and midnight movie madness, reminiscent of early David Lynch and the splatterpunks at their most sublime. **172 pages $11**

BB-124 **"Black Hole Blues" Patrick Wensink** — A hilarious double helix of country music and physics. **196 pages $11**

BB-125 **"Barbarian Beast Bitches of the Badlands" Carlton Mellick III** — Three prequels and sequels to *Warrior Wolf Women of the Wasteland*. **284 pages $13**

BB-126 **"The Traveling Dildo Salesman" Kevin L. Donihe** — A nightmare comedy about destiny, faith, and sex toys. Also featuring Donihe's most lurid and infamous short stories: *Milky Agitation, Two-Way Santa, The Helen Mower, Living Room Zombies*, and *Revenge of the Living Masturbation Rag*. **108 pages $8**

BB-127 **"Metamorphosis Blues" Bruce Taylor** — Enter a land of love beasts, intergalactic cowboys, and rock 'n roll. A land where Sears Catalogs are doorways to insanity and men keep mysterious black boxes. Welcome to the monstrous mind of Mr. Magic Realism. **136 pages $11**

BB-128 **"The Driver's Guide to Hitting Pedestrians" Andersen Prunty** — A pocket guide to the twenty-three most painful things in life, written by the most well-adjusted man in the universe. **108 pages $8**

BB-129 **"Island of the Super People" Kevin Shamel** — Four students and their anthropology professor journey to a remote island to study its indigenous population. But this is no ordinary native culture. They're super heroes and villains with flesh costumes and outlandish abilities like self-detonation, musical eyelashes, and microwave hands. **194 pages $11**

BB-130 **"Fantastic Orgy" Carlton Mellick III** — Shark Sex, mutant cats, and strange sexually transmitted diseases. Featuring the stories: *Candy-coated, Ear Cat, Fantastic Orgy, City Hobgoblins*, and *Porno in August*. **136 pages $9**

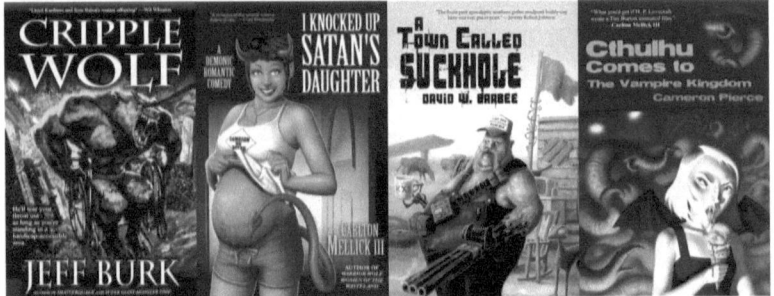

BB-131 **"Cripple Wolf" Jeff Burk** — Part man. Part wolf. 100% crippled. Also including *Punk Rock Nursing Home, Adrift with Space Badgers, Cook for Your Life, Just Another Day in the Park, Frosty and the Full Monty*, and *House of Cats*. **152 pages $10**

BB-132 **"I Knocked Up Satan's Daughter" Carlton Mellick III** — An adorable, violent, fantastical love story. A romantic comedy for the bizarro fiction reader. **152 pages $10**

BB-133 **"A Town Called Suckhole" David W. Barbee** — Far into the future, in the nuclear bowels of post-apocalyptic Dixie, there is a town. A town of derelict mobile homes, ancient junk, and mutant wildlife. A town of slack jawed rednecks who bask in the splendors of moonshine and mud boggin'. A town dedicated to the bloody and demented legacy of the Old South. A town called Suckhole. **144 pages $10**

BB-134 **"Cthulhu Comes to the Vampire Kingdom" Cameron Pierce** — What you'd get if H. P. Lovecraft wrote a Tim Burton animated film. **148 pages $11**

BB-135 **"I am Genghis Cum" Violet LeVoit** — From the savage Arctic tundra to post-partum mutations to your missing daughter's unmarked grave, join visionary madwoman Violet LeVoit in this non-stop eight-story onslaught of full-tilt Bizarro punk lit thrills. **124 pages $9**

BB-136 **"Haunt" Laura Lee Bahr** — A tripping-balls Los Angeles noir, where a mysterious dame drags you through a time-warping Bizarro hall of mirrors. **316 pages $13**

BB-137 **"Amazing Stories of the Flying Spaghetti Monster" edited by Cameron Pierce** — Like an all-spaghetti evening of Adult Swim, the Flying Spaghetti Monster will show you the many realms of His Noodly Appendage. Learn of those who worship him and the lives he touches in distant, mysterious ways. **228 pages $12**

BB-138 **"Wave of Mutilation" Douglas Lain** — A dream-pop exploration of modern architecture and the American identity, *Wave of Mutilation* is a Zen finger trap for the 21st century. **100 pages $8**

BB-139 **"Hooray for Death!" Mykle Hansen** — Famous Author Mykle Hansen draws unconventional humor from deaths tiny and large, and invites you to laugh while you can. **128 pages $10**

BB-140 **"Hypno-hog's Moonshine Monster Jamboree" Andrew Goldfarb** — Hicks, Hogs, Horror! Goldfarb is back with another strange illustrated tale of backwoods weirdness. **120 pages $9**

BB-141 **"Broken Piano For President" Patrick Wensink** — A comic masterpiece about the fast food industry, booze, and the necessity to choose happiness over work and security. **372 pages $15**

BB-142 **"Please Do Not Shoot Me in the Face" Bradley Sands** — A novel in three parts, *Please Do Not Shoot Me in the Face: A Novel*, is the story of one boy detective, the worst ninja in the world, and the great American fast food wars. It is a novel of loss, destruction, and--incredibly--genuine hope. **224 pages $12**

BB-143 **"Santa Steps Out" Robert Devereaux** — Sex, Death, and Santa Claus ... The ultimate erotic Christmas story is back. **294 pages $13**

BB-144 **"Santa Conquers the Homophobes" Robert Devereaux** — "I wish I could hope to ever attain one-thousandth the perversity of Robert Devereaux's toenail clippings." - Poppy Z. Brite **316 pages $13**

BB-145 **"We Live Inside You" Jeremy Robert Johnson** — "Jeremy Robert Johnson is dancing to a way different drummer. He loves language, he loves the edge, and he loves us people. These stories have range and style and wit. This is entertainment... and literature."- Jack Ketchum **188 pages $11**

BB-146 **"Clockwork Girl" Athena Villaverde** — Urban fairy tales for the weird girl in all of us. Like a combination of Francesca Lia Block, Charles de Lint, Kathe Koja, Tim Burton, and Hayao Miyazaki, her stories are cute, kinky, edgy, magical, provocative, and strange, full of poetic imagery and vicious sexuality. **160 pages $10**

BB-147 **"Armadillo Fists" Carlton Mellick III** — A weird-as-hell gangster story set in a world where people drive giant mechanical dinosaurs instead of cars. **168 pages $11**

BB-148 **"Gargoyle Girls of Spider Island" Cameron Pierce** — Four college seniors venture out into open waters for the tropical party weekend of a life-time. Instead of a teenage sex fantasy, they find themselves in a nightmare of pirates, sharks, and sex-crazed monsters. **100 pages $8**

BB-149 **"The Handsome Squirm" by Carlton Mellick III** — Like Franz Kafka's *The Trial* meets an erotic body horror version of *The Blob*. **158 pages $11**

BB-150 **"Tentacle Death Trip" Jordan Krall** — It's *Death Race 2000* meets H. P. Lovecraft in bizarro author Jordan Krall's best and most suspenseful work to date. **224 pages $12**

BB-151 **"The Obese" Nick Antosca** — Like Alfred Hitchcock's *The Birds*... but with obese people. **108 pages $10**

BB-152 **"All-Monster Action!" Cody Goodfellow** — The world gave him a blank check and a demand: Create giant monsters to fight our wars. But Dr. Otaku was not satisfied with mere chaos and mass destruction.... **216 pages $12**

BB-153 **"Ugly Heaven" Carlton Mellick III** — Heaven is no longer a para-dise. It was once a blissful utopia full of wonders far beyond human comprehension. But the afterlife is now in ruins. It has become an ugly, lonely wasteland populated by strange monstrous beasts, masturbating angels, and sad man-like beings wallowing in the remains of the once-great Kingdom of God. **106 pages $8**

BB-154 **"Space Walrus" Kevin L. Donihe** — Walter is supposed to go where no walrus has ever gone before, but all this astronaut walrus really wants is to take it easy on the intense training, escape the chimpanzee bullies, and win the love of his human trainer Dr. Stephanie. **160 pages $11**

BB-155 **"Unicorn Battle Squad" Kirsten Alene** — Mutant unicorns. A palace with a thousand human legs. The most powerful army on the planet. **192 pages $11**

BB-156 **"Kill Ball" Carlton Mellick III** — In a city where all humans live inside of plastic bubbles, exotic dancers are being murdered in the rubbery streets by a mysterious stalker known only as Kill Ball. **134 pages $10**

BB-157 **"Die You Doughnut Bastards" Cameron Pierce** — The bacon storm is rolling in. We hear the grease and sugar beat against the roof and windows. The doughnut people are attacking. We press close together, forgetting for a moment that we hate each other. **196 pages $11**

BB-158 **"Tumor Fruit" Carlton Mellick III** — Eight desperate castaways find themselves stranded on a mysterious deserted island. They are surrounded by poisonous blue plants and an ocean made of acid. Ravenous creatures lurk in the toxic jungle. The ghostly sound of crying babies can be heard on the wind. **310 pages $13**

BB-159 **"Thunderpussy" David W. Barbee** — When it comes to high-tech global espionage, only one man has the balls to save humanity from the world's most powerful bastards. He's Declan Magpie Bruce, Agent 00X. **136 pages $11**

BB-160 **"Papier Mâché Jesus" Kevin L. Donihe** — Donihe's surreal wit and beautiful mind-bending imagination is on full display with stories such as All Children Go to Hell, Happiness is a Warm Gun, and Swimming in Endless Night. **154 pages $11**

BB-161 **"Cuddly Holocaust" Carlton Mellick III** — The war between humans and toys has come to an end. The toys won. **172 pages $11**

BB-162 **"Hammer Wives" Carlton Mellick III** — Fish-eyed mutants, oceans of insects, and flesh-eating women with hammers for heads. Hammer Wives collects six of his most popular novelettes and short stories. **152 pages $10**